LOVE AND BRUISES

K.J. Ersti

For the girls who are happily with a golden retriever but like their MMCs a little unhinged.

1

Art

"You can go in now, Mr. Michaels."

I nodded, but my feet refused to budge from where they were rooted in the hospital hallway. I knew what to expect from what I'd been told, but how ready is anybody to see a dead body, especially one that you used to call family?

The nurse continued to stand awkwardly beside me, and I finally loosened my feet enough to enter the room.

It seemed like everyone had strong feelings about hospitals, but I had never really been in one long enough to develop any sort of opinions.

My first impression of the room was quiet. Eerily quiet. In TV shows, you'd hear beeping and machines whirring, but this room was dead silent. I was pretty sure the AC unit wasn't even running. Then again, in TV shows, hospitals were mostly focused on keeping people alive, not housing the dead.

My mother lay in a hospital bed, a white sheet pulled up to her chest and her hands laid straight on either side of her body. It had been a couple months since I'd seen her last, but she looked the same. Dyed burgundy hair lay neatly on her pillow as though someone had just combed it for her. With her amount of wealth, they probably had. Or maybe that was something they did for all the recently deceased.

There was a chair pulled up next to the bed as if someone had been sitting next to her. Or maybe it was for me. I felt weird just standing over her, so I sat down, keeping my eyes on her face. I expected her to look different. To feel somehow different. Instead, she looked like she was about to open her eyes and say *"Sike! Now hand me my planner so I can get back to work."*

I didn't know what to do or say. I'd never really contemplated my mom's death before. Maybe I'd always assumed she'd be a gray old lady in a nursing home when I came to say my last goodbye. Although I really couldn't picture her old or gray. I guess now she never would be.

I was sad about her passing, but honestly, I wasn't heartbroken, and I felt like the worst son, because who could look at their dead mom and not feel anything?

It wasn't like we'd had a toxic relationship. She'd never hit me or even emotionally abused me. She just wasn't there. She'd been so focused on creating her empire that I took a backseat, and when I'd gotten old enough, I had left home and never looked back. I took full advantage of the money and status she provided, but I could count on one hand how many meaningful memories I had with her.

Honestly, the hardest part of all this was the fact that I would now be responsible for taking over her hugely successful hotel franchise as CEO. I'd spent so long aimlessly wandering through life, partying, going where I wanted, and acting on every whim that the idea of boardrooms, conference calls, data and numbers seemed stifling.

"Not that I'm blaming you. It's not like you asked to die an early death," I murmured, breaking the silence of the room.

Guilt hit me at the thought, which was quickly replaced with embarrassment. I was talking to a dead body.

I leaned forward but couldn't make myself touch her hand. "Goodbye, Mother. Thanks for all of your hard work. I'll try to live up to your legacy."

With that, I stood and exited the room. A nurse stood outside talking to several people in suits, including Cain, my mother's COO. I nodded at them.

"You know how to get ahold of me if you need to."

He grunted in what sounded like disappointment, but I couldn't care less what he or anyone else thought about my short-lived goodbye. It was no one else's business what my relationship with my mother had been, and they were all better suited to handle the funeral details and whatever else came next. Besides, I needed a strong drink. Or two.

2

Ava

I swirled my glass and watched the ice mix with the mint leaves before glancing around the expensive bar again. Out of all the places I had been sent for work, this was one of the nicest. I didn't have a lot of experience staying in nice hotels, but even if I had been a world traveler, this place would have been impressive.

The Laurie was part of a chain of luxury hotels scattered across the country, and its New York location was particularly impressive. The atmosphere dripped wealth and comfort, with overstuffed leather couches, cushioned bar stools, and dimly lit crystal chandeliers. The hotel was way out of my budget as an up-and-coming journalist; however, my newest interview was to take place here, so my stay was comped, and I was going to enjoy every minute of it.

"Is this seat taken?"

I pulled myself from my musings and took in the tall, dark-haired man in front of me. If I had to guess he was in his mid to late twenties. Like most of the other men here, he wore a custom, tailored suit, but his trimmed beard and piercing blue eyes set him apart.

I nodded my head at the empty stool. "It's all yours."

He slid onto the seat and stuck his hand out. "I'm Art."

"Ava." I shook his hand. It was strong, firm, and he held it for a second longer than normal.

"Beautiful."

I felt a blush climb up my face as I ducked my head, taking a sip of my drink. After another sip of liquid courage, I turned back to see him staring at me with his drink to his lips.

"Are you in town for business?" I inquired.

He nodded, setting his drink back on the bar. "How could you tell?"

"I dunno, the charcoal suit and trying to pick up women at the bar might have been a clue."

He let out a deep laugh and the sound sent butterflies straight to my stomach.

"What about you?" he asked.

I swirled my drink again. "Yep, and I'm planning on taking advantage of all of the amenities on my company's dime."

"*All* of them?" he questioned, looking at me over the rim of his glass. The fire in my belly spread at the warmth in his gaze. I wasn't usually the type to let myself be seduced by strangers, but after my third mojito…

"Depends on how interesting I find them." What was I saying? *Mental note, stop drinking in public, Ava.*

He finally set his glass down, turning the full force of his attention on me. "Let me be your tour guide. I can show you all of the most *interesting* amenities."

If it wasn't for the alcohol hazing my brain, I would have found his pickup lines extremely cheesy, but with my blood feeling lazy and tingly, his offer brought images of stolen kisses and dark promises. I forged ahead before I could stop myself.

"Married?"

"Single."

"Felon?"

He smirked. "Negative."

"Okay then." When I sobered up, I really needed to revisit the fact that my list of qualifications was so short.

He leaned toward me and, when I didn't make a move to retreat, gently tucked a strand of my short hair behind my ear.

"You gonna finish your drink?" he asked softly.

"I probably should," I murmured. "Company's money and all that."

His hand moved down to my shoulder as he dragged his fingertips lightly against my bare arm.

"Of course, you wouldn't want to waste their money."

I didn't even know what we were saying anymore, I was too focused on the warmth spreading through my body and the electricity crackling between us. My breath hitched when his hand began tracing lines along my thigh. Even through my jeans, his touch left a trail of heat in its wake.

"You have a room here?" he asked.

I nodded, chugging the rest of my rum and lime, the mint leaves sticking to the ice left in the tumbler. When I looked back at him, his glass was also empty, and he offered me his hand. I hesitated for a second. Did I really want to hook up with someone I had met thirty seconds ago?

Yes was the surprising answer.

I didn't know what it was about him that attracted me like a bee to honey, but whatever it was, I didn't want to fight it or try to reason with it tonight. It had been a stressful couple months and a long time since I had been with someone. Tonight, I just wanted to forget it all and feel good. For some reason, looking at Art, I thought that he could accomplish that.

I placed my palm in his still outstretched hand, and he helped me slide off my stool, placing several bills on the counter before tugging me toward the elevator. Once he stepped inside, he looked at the buttons expectantly. *Oh yeah, my room.*

"Twenty three," I said, and he pressed the button, then turned back toward me, and I felt a rush at the intensity in his stare. His gaze roamed from my short blonde hair that fell above my shoulders, snagged on my mouth, and then trailed down my breasts and over my hips. I hadn't dressed for any particular occasion this morning, choosing one of my favorite camisoles and a pair of jeans that hugged my curves just right.

He took two steps forward, closing the distance between us, leaned down, and without a word, his lips met mine. They were soft yet firm, and he kissed with purpose. He tasted like mint and whiskey, and I loved how he had to lean down to kiss me.

I opened up for him when his tongue ran along the seam of my lips and groaned into his mouth when his tongue continued his exploration, his body pressed firmly against mine, pushing me into the wall behind me.

My hands roamed up his back, into his short dark hair before tugging his head further toward me. He obliged without resistance.

The elevator dinged and the doors opened to my floor. I was breathing heavy and my clit throbbed. I could only imagine what we looked like, hair messed and lips swollen. If anyone had been waiting outside, it would have been obvious what they were interrupting.

Thankfully, no one was there, and I exited the elevator on shaky legs with Art following close enough behind that I could feel his warmth on my back. We reached my room, and I slid my key card in before the door unlocked with a beep and I pushed my way in.

When I had first checked-in, I had just set my suitcases inside before heading down to the bar, so the room was still untouched. The door opened into a suite with a couch, table, and small kitchenette. To the left sat the single bedroom with a king bed. More than I needed, but when someone else was paying...

The door closed behind us, and I turned to see Art stalk toward me without even a glance at the room. My breath caught when he marched me back to the wall, caging me in with his hands on either side of my head. Apparently I wasn't the only one in need of a quick release. The kiss in the elevator had been a spark that ignited an inferno between us.

Art grabbed the back of my neck and pulled my mouth back to his. I moaned at the dominance in his touch. I had never been kissed like this before, and I never wanted it to end. Suddenly, his hands were beneath my thighs as he lifted and carried me through the bedroom door, his erection pressing into me, and I squirmed against him for more friction.

"Careful," he murmured into my neck.

We reached the bed, and he dropped me onto the comforter, stopping to slip out of his suit jacket. He filled out his white dress shirt as if it were made for him, which it probably was, with broad shoulders and muscular arms noticeable even through the crisp fabric. He reached for my cami, and I let him slip it up over my head, a twinge of self-consciousness flaring up as he assessed my shirtless torso, but the heat in his gaze and the resulting smirk that curved his mouth told me what he thought of the sight.

"Stunning," he said as he gently pushed me back to the bed, pinning my body with his. I moaned at the feeling of his weight on top of me, his erection rubbing against my pants. He pulled back and I instantly missed the feel of him, though his hands explored my back, unlatching my strapless bra as he continued to kiss me. Our limbs became a tangle of pulling and twisting as we quickly undressed each other down to our underwear.

When I was left in only my thong, he stepped back and began leaving a trail of kisses over my legs. I sucked in a breath as his hot breath came closer and closer to my center, pressing a kiss to my inner thigh, and all I could do was pant, "Art."

He pulled back enough to smirk at me. "Is there something you want, Ava?"

I didn't answer, just lifted my hips in invitation. He pressed my hips back into the bed and tsked, "So impatient," before continuing his slow trek to my other thigh. I tried to buck against him, but again he held me firm, placing a kiss to my thong, and I gasped, "Fuck."

He let out a dark chuckle as he finally pulled my underwear off, looking up at me through thick lashes, and gave me a long, slow lick.

"Oh my god," I cried, as I arched off the bed.

"Why thank you, but Art will do."

I couldn't even process his snarky comment as he continued to feast on me. My orgasm began to build low in my stomach while he continued licking and sucking. He pressed a kiss to my clit, causing my eyes to roll into the back of my head, and I moaned, "Fuck me."

"Working on it, love."

I grunted in response and the answering chuckle against my core sent me over the edge. I came with a shout, and he continued kissing me until my body stilled.

Finally, he shifted back, sliding his boxers off, and I watched in appreciation as he pulled himself free and took out a condom.

"Like what you see there, little bird?"

"You talk too much," I muttered at his cockiness.

He let out another laugh and climbed back on top of me. "I'm sorry, are you not enjoying the experience?" he asked with a raised brow.

I halfheartedly pushed against his chest, but he leaned in and captured my mouth again. I kissed him back and rocked my hips against him, desperate for more, and he groaned as his cock slid against my wet center before pushing himself inside me. We swallowed each other's moans as his cock stretched me and I tightened around him.

"Fuck, Ava, you feel so fucking good."

I moaned in response, matching his thrusts with my own. Another orgasm started low in my stomach at the sensation of him filling me, hitting those spots, but it wasn't enough.

"Harder," I grunted.

He stilled and I wanted to whine at the lack of friction.

"What do you want?"

"Harder," I repeated.

"I'm sorry, harder what?"

"Oh my god. Please, Art, will you please fuck me harder?"

He grinned at my sass. "Only 'cause you asked so nicely." He pulled out to the tip and thrust into me savagely.

"Fuck!" I shouted and he kept going until another orgasm exploded out of me. His thrusts became sloppier, more erratic, and then he too was grunting as he came. After a moment, he rolled off me and we both lay there panting.

"That was… nice," I murmured.

"Hmmm," he said, and I glanced to my side to see him staring at me appreciatively. My heart skipped a beat at the thought that he found me so attractive. I was a relationship type of person. Rarely did anyone I wasn't comfortable around see me naked. I was working on my self-confidence, but, even still, accepting all of my rolls and stretch marks was a work in progress.

I went to use the bathroom, and when I came back, he was leaning against the headboard, typing on his phone with a frown. I slid under the fresh sheets, feeling the alcohol and post-orgasm haze drag me toward sleep.

"I'm assuming you can find your way out of here?"

He finally glanced up from his phone. "Rude. Kicking me out already?"

I rolled my eyes. "My day started way earlier than I would have liked. I need to get some sleep before work again tomorrow."

"Can I at least get your phone number?"

I paused. Did I want to share it with him and create the possibility of more of this? *Yes.*

After he typed it into his phone, he finally slid off the bed, and I watched him find his clothes, putting his undershirt and dress pants back on before draping his jacket over his arm.

"Thanks for the sex, Ava."

I rolled my eyes again. "You're oh *so* welcome, Art."

He smirked, leaving the room without another word, the door clicking shut behind him before I rolled onto my side.

Not a bad end to the day.

3

Art

I woke up to a pounding headache and the taste of Ava on my tongue. The first made me want to throw my phone across the room and the second to go finish what we started last night.

I groaned and forced myself to turn off my alarm without breaking anything. Then, with bleary vision, I pulled up her contact from last night and typed out a message.

Good morning, beautiful, I can still taste you in my beard.

I didn't really expect a response, at least not right away, but my phone alerted me to a new message, and I laughed when I read it.

Oh my god, I think that might be the creepiest text I've ever gotten. Blocking this number now.

What are you doing right now?

Trying to prepare for a work meeting. You?

Trying to get the willpower not to go back to sleep. I know something that could help wake me up.

Please stop before I call the police.

I didn't know you were an exhibitionist but go off.
I hate you.
What are you doing later?
Not you.
Ouch.

I laughed again as I forced myself to finally sit up. She might act like she didn't want to see me, but she had mentioned that she was here for work, so I was pretty sure I could find some time when she would be free after she was off the clock.

When she didn't respond, I pulled on a robe and shuffled out of my room and into the dining area, where the table was already set with steaming plates of breakfast items, including eggs, sausage, hash browns, and bowls of fruit, courtesy of Angie, my all in one housekeeper and cook.

I slid into a chair, serving myself from the feast before me, but before I could enjoy my first bite, a knock sounded on the door and then it was being pushed open. I scowled at the doorway where the only person brazen enough to let himself in without being invited stood. Cain. He approached me without a hint of remorse, settling into a spot across from me at the table.

"I'm so glad to see you're up. I was a little worried I'd have to pull you out of bed myself."

I grunted at him and poured myself some coffee with a healthy dose of creamer. He continued as if I wasn't staring daggers at him and his obnoxiously loud voice.

"The board will be here in half an hour, I already have a conference room set up for it. There's still some paperwork you need to look over before we go, and several of the more pressing documents require your signature before we can send them off."

I groaned, rubbing my temples. I really shouldn't have visited the bar last night. But then again, if I hadn't gone down there, I wouldn't have run into Ava. The thought of her brought some light to what would otherwise be a shitty day. After the meeting, I would have to get something sent to her room. Maybe an invite to dinner.

That sounded good, give us a chance to talk, and then maybe we could go back to my room tonight. I knew next to nothing about her, but last night had been amazing, and I could use some more stress relief. It had been a shitty week.

"The Manhattan Press is sending someone over for the board meeting as we—are you even listening to me?" Cain asked, irritation lacing his question.

"Hm? Yeah, thanks, Cain, I trust you've got it handled."

The look on his face was less than pleased, but I didn't particularly care. Cain had been on staff with my mom for decades, and not many people knew the ins and outs of the business better than him.

While the transition of CEO from my mom, may she rest in peace, to me might have a lot of signatures required, none of it was too much for Cain to handle. He didn't need me micromanaging. The fact that my mom had passed so unexpectedly left us scrambling to get all the logistics in place. Rephrase that, left *them* scrambling and me drowning my anxiety in alcohol and sex. What else was new?

Cain left without another word, and I meandered back into my room. I had stayed in this penthouse many times before, but this was generally where my mother stayed, and because of that, I had always preferred to find alternative housing. Now that this would be my home base, I needed to officially move in. I had brought over a few bags of items so far, and the movers would be bringing the rest of my stuff over today.

The thought of my mom brought a weird feeling to my chest, a conflicting lack of grief along with a touch of rebellion for what lay ahead. Because of her death, my life as I knew it was now over. Not that my life had been a terrible thing, but I was aware of enough of the gossip to know that my reputation as a drunken playboy wasn't going to do great things for the company's image.

I finished getting dressed and made my way toward the conference room, taking the elevator down several floors and entering the large space with floor to ceiling windows. There were already several board members present, some I knew by name, others who were only vaguely familiar.

I sat down in my mother's seat—*my seat*, I reminded myself—and reached for the coffee that was already at my spot, curtesy of Jane, my mother's—*my* assistant. Cain sat to my right, talking to another board member, and I perused the room while I waited for everyone else to arrive.

A couple more people trickled in, and I was about to flag Jane down for another coffee, when a flash of white caught my attention by the door. Ava walked into the room, deeply engrossed in conversation with an older lady I hadn't seen before. They both took seats at the end of the table, and I wracked my brain trying to figure out why on earth she would be here.

She still hadn't looked up at me, and I took advantage of the opportunity to soak her in. Her short hair was slightly curled, and she wore a cream sweater and black dress pants that put her curvy body on display. She looked beautiful, but nothing close to the perfection of her lying naked in her bed last night with a sated smile on her face, or when her body arched underneath my touch as I—

"I think we're all here," Cain's voice broke through my daydreams. I kept my gaze on Ava as she finally turned to look up at me, and I caught the flash of surprise that crossed her face along with a slight pink flush of her cheeks. Cain continued to drone on, but all I could do was stare as one sentence ran in repeat in my brain, *why are you here?*

"I want to thank Ms. Parly and Ms. Schmidt from the

Manhattan Press for joining us today, we're hoping to smooth our working relationship moving forward."

The woman next to Ava nodded her head at the acknowledgment, and surprise rocked through me. The *Manhattan Press*. Ava was from the *Manhattan Press*?

"We know some people have their concerns with the suddenness of CEO change; however, we want the public to rest assured that the Laurie is in good hands and the safety and comfort of our guests remain our top priority."

Cain had mentioned something about inviting reporters from the *Manhattan Press* to the board meeting in an attempt to help my image after an offending article had been published, but I hadn't read it yet. I tuned him out as I opened my phone and typed in '*Manhattan Press* Laurie.' The first article popped up within seconds.

Professional or Playboy?

After the unfortunate passing of CEO Laurie Michaels of Laurie hotels, the fate of the hotel franchise rests in the hands of Arthur Michaels, Laurie's only son. The known playboy has spent more of his 27 years chasing skirts rather than wearing suits, so what does this mean for the future of the franchise?

I skimmed the article and read the name at the bottom. Ava Schmidt. My head began pounding in earnest, and I looked up to see Ava staring intently at Cain.

Fuck. Her.

4

Ava

Of all the guys I had to run into in a hotel bar and bring back to my room, I stumbled on Arther freaking Michaels.

"Are you in town for business?"

"How could you guess?"

He *owned* the freaking hotel. He was my current job. I was here to write a piece on him, dig into his past, find and publish every reason he was going to make this franchise fail. Oh, and I just casually fucked him before the first interview.

Stupid, stupid, stupid, I berated myself.

"If that's alright with you, Ms. Parly," Cain, the Laurie's COO was saying to my boss. I tried to rein my thoughts back in as she nodded, and I realized I had no idea what they were talking about. Shit. I really needed to get my head in the game and pay better attention. Kim liked me well enough, but I knew there were a dozen people waiting for me to fail so that they could have this article and move themselves up in the ranks. Eat or be eaten, as they said.

I focused my attention back on Cain and made a conscious

effort to avoid looking toward Art. Arthur, whatever his name was. He looked good this morning. A little tired, a little less chipper, but just as attractive as he had been last night.

The shock on his face reflected how I was feeling. Out of everyone I was expecting to see, last night's one night stand was not on the list.

In the brief research I'd done so far on him, I hadn't seen a picture. I was expecting a stuck-up rich kid, not whatever I'd experienced last night.

It was great sex, that was it, I told myself.

And this morning? I'd been pleasantly surprised to hear from him again so soon and had been tempted to try to plan something again for tonight.

The shuffling of papers once again pulled me out of my thoughts, and I finally allowed myself to look over at Art. Cain handed him papers, which he signed, and flashes went off as multiple pictures were taken.

Hello, world, meet Arthur, the new CEO of Laurie hotels and my latest one-night stand.

I ground my teeth in an attempt to shut up my inner monologue as he passed the last paper to Cain. Then he looked up and our gazes met. His eyes looked cold and disinterested as they passed over me in a matter of seconds. A pang went through me, and if I didn't know better, I'd think he didn't even remember me from last night. But that wasn't right, because his shock had been clear when he first saw me enter the room.

"It would be wise to introduce ourselves," Kim said as she stood. I followed behind her without a word, and in a moment we were standing in front of him. Art shook the hand of the man he was talking to before turning to look at us.

He stuck out his hand to Kim, "Arthur Michaels."

"Kim Parly, thank you for having us today, and

congratulations on your promotion."

He nodded, seeming to have as little interest in us as he did the carpet pattern, and then Kim put her hand on my back and pushed me forward a step.

"This is Ava Schmidt, a junior journalist and the one who will be taking point on the interviews."

He finally turned his gaze to me, and my lungs squeezed at what I saw there. Gone was the warmth and teasing of last night. There was nothing remotely friendly in his gaze as he nodded at me with a brief, "Arthur."

I cleared my throat, because the silence felt suffocating, and Kim appeared to be waiting for me to say something.

"I look forward to talking more with you in the future."

His glare could have frozen a volcano.

"If you'll excuse me," he said in a clipped tone before abruptly leaving. I swallowed past the dryness in my throat as Kim mumbled under her breath, "Real piece of work that one."

What had I gotten myself into?

5

Murderer

I hated dead bodies. The way that they looked, smelled, didn't move even when you poked and prodded them. I didn't relish any of this. The man who lay on the bed before me with a bullet in his head was no different. He had simply been a means to an end.

I peeled the gloves off of my hands and tucked them into my pants pocket, leaving a second pair of gloves underneath. I had drugged him before shooting him, and by some luck, he'd ended up in bed before I got here, saving me from having to drag him there myself.

All in all, it had been a pretty clean kill, and I walked around the scene to double check that it was perfect before I left.

I had used the gun because I needed it to be an obvious murder, but nothing about it should tie back to me. He had enough enemies that it wouldn't be all that surprising to find him dead. That wasn't the important part. The investigation should lead nowhere, and I wasn't attempting to pin it on anyone. Just the fact that he was murdered here should do the trick.

Arthur Michaels needed to know that no one in this hotel was safe. The public needed to be aware that there wasn't a thing that he could do to protect them, even right under his nose. Being born into wealth didn't give you the ability to run a company, and that spoiled brat was no exception.

Satisfied that everything was how I wanted it, I did one last sweep before exiting the bedroom, making sure that the do not disturb sign was off the door as I left. I would deal with the hallway cameras next and then leave it to housekeeping to alert the staff of this poor excuse of a hotel.

6

Art

The next morning, I was in my office for the first time as CEO, when Jane announced, "Mr. Michaels, there's somebody from the coroner's office on the phone for you."

"Thank you." I didn't know how long it would take me to get used to having a personal assistant, but I definitely wasn't there yet.

"Michaels," I answered the call.

"Hello, this is Mason with the coroner's office calling for Arthur Michaels."

"This is Arthur."

"Thank you for taking my call, I'm calling about the results of your mother's autopsy report."

My heart rate sped up at his words. When I had first been called about her death, all they knew was that it had been sudden and unexpected. Possibly a heart attack or stroke. She was still fairly young and healthy, so it was definitely a surprise, but there was any number of things that could have caused it.

"After completing the autopsy, your mother's death was ruled as hypersensitivity due to Botox injection," he continued.

"Excuse me?"

"Based on the clinical findings, Ms. Michales appears to have had some sort of reaction to her most recent Botox injection. While Botox is generally a very safe procedure, there have been a few rare cases of severe reaction, and it appears that is what caused your mother's death."

I was stunned. My mother died because of Botox? Her life just ended because she was trying to look younger?

I realized that the line had gone quiet, and I didn't know what to say. Did you thank someone for telling you your mother's cause of death? That just felt wrong.

"Are you still there, Mr. Michaels?"

"Yes."

"Is there anything else I can do for you?"

"No, thank you."

"Her body is being released to the morgue in preparation for the funeral, please let us know if we can help in any other way."

I had no idea how else they expected to help, what other services could a coroner provide me? I kept those thoughts to myself as I ended the call and dialed up my best friend. I was in desperate need of a release. Either the boxing ring or shooting range. I would let Finn pick.

# # #

"The audacity," I grunted as I threw another punch toward Finn's head. He easily ducked my blow, spun under my arm, and tapped my back with his pads.

"So you've said."

"I don't know why you're not on my side about this," I said

with another swing.

He took a step back and raised his eyebrows at me, "Maybe because it sounds like she's just doing her job?"

"Yeah, if her job is to drag my name through the mud and make me look as incompetent as possible."

"She's a journalist, I'm pretty sure that's her exact job description," he said with a laugh, causing his orange curls to bounce.

We didn't speak again until we finished the match, taking off our gloves and stepping out of the ring.

"Honestly, I don't understand why Cain thinks it'll be a good idea to do an official interview with the very magazine that already published the article. It's not like they're going to come out and retract the piece," I said, wiping the sweat off my neck with a towel.

"Who the hell knows," Finn said. "I'm just your friendly neighborhood cop, that stuff is way above my pay grade."

I rolled my eyes at his snark as my phone alerted me to a message and I glanced briefly at it before stifling a groan. "Speak of the devil."

"She has your number?"

"No, well, yes, but it's Cain letting me know when and where to meet her. You gonna help a guy out if she mysteriously goes missing?"

Finn swatted my arm, "You've gotta stop saying stuff like that. But also, yes."

I laughed and clapped him on the shoulder. "I'll let you know how it goes and which one of us ends up alive."

I grabbed the rest of my stuff and headed for the exit. When I had first left home for college, the press had had a field day following me and recording all of my teenage mishaps and exploits. My name was flashed on the front page of articles more times than I could count. The only son of an entrepreneur and businesswoman the public loved, traipsing around and disgracing her every chance he got.

They had finally moved onto more interesting topics, but seeing Ava's article had brought it all back. I knew I'd never done anything worthwhile, and I didn't have a lot of direction, but what else was I supposed to do when I knew I'd be inheriting my mom's multimillion dollar business? I'd skated by in school to get a business degree and was just passing time until I was supposed to start working in the family business. Little did I know it would be so soon. And now the press was back to make sure everyone witnessed every single mistake.

I ground my teeth as I turned out of the parking garage of the studio where Finn and I often boxed. I had been so excited about meeting a gorgeous woman I had great chemistry with, as, contrary to what everyone said about me, my love life was all too boring most of the time. And of course she had to sweep in and get me excited just to turn out to be a conniving—

A car pulling out in front of me in traffic cut off my ranting as I turned my attention to the road and the brief drive back to the Laurie. Cain had reserved another one of the conference rooms for this interview with Ava, and I parked before taking the elevator to the tenth floor.

When I entered the conference room, I noticed that Ava was already seated facing the doorway, staring down at her phone. She glanced up as I entered, and I schooled my features into a practiced mask. Her boss wasn't here today, so it would just be the two of us. Great.

I slid into a seat across the table from her, and within seconds Jane entered with my usual coffee. She had a second cup for Ava and after setting them down, ducked out of the room. I picked up my cup and held her stare. I had nothing to say, let her make the first move.

She cleared her throat, "So, Art is short for Arthur."

I raised an eyebrow, "I can see how you became a journalist, very astute."

Her polite stare turned a shade colder. "I didn't expect the CEO to be picking up girls in the lobby."

I leaned back in my chair comfortably. "First off, I wasn't technically CEO that night. Secondly, what *did* you expect me to be doing? Shuffling papers? Going to bed early?" *And alone*, hung in the space between us.

Her gaze dropped to my mouth and my muscles tightened as I imagined her replaying what it felt like to have my mouth tracing every one of her curves.

She cleared her throat again, "Anyway, we should get back to the interview."

I set my cup back on the table and continued to stare in silence as she looked down at what I presumed were some notes in front of her.

"When did you move back to New York?"

"I've been bouncing between New York and Chicago for a while now, I have places in both, so it really wasn't a huge move."

She nodded and looked like she was about to ask another question when she changed her mind and said, "I'm sorry about your mom."

I shrugged. "So, why'd you write that piece on me?"

She blinked like she was taken aback. "Oh, um, The Laurie has been getting a lot of publicity recently," she said as if that answer was enough.

"So why not profit off of that by attempting to smear my name everywhere, huh?"

Before she had a chance to reply, my phone vibrated, pulling my gaze from hers and saving her from thinking up some bullshit excuse.

Jackson. *Meet me in your penthouse immediately.* I frowned. There weren't many reasons the hotel's head of security would request my immediate presence. I pocketed my phone and stood.

"Well, as thrilling as this conversation has been, I have a situation that needs my attention."

Ava stood as well and gathered her papers in front of her.

"Of course," she said in a tight voice. I honestly didn't care how irritated this made her. The interruption might have just saved me from one of the most miserable conversations I'd had in a long while. I walked toward the elevator, and she followed behind stiffly.

As I pressed the floor for my penthouse and scanned my card, she murmured,

"Twenty three, please."

I nodded and glanced her way, biting my tongue to remark that I did indeed remember that from our time in her room. A pink tinge took over her cheeks as she held my gaze, and I knew she too was thinking about our evening together.

Despite myself, my gaze strayed to her pink lips, which were parted just the smallest bit. God I wanted to taste her again, reach down and feel the silkiness of her skin, push her against the wall of the elevator and feel her legs wrap around my waist.

I took a step toward her and watched her pulse flutter in her throat as I tucked a stray piece of her hair behind her ear and leaned closer. She smelled like vanilla and cinnamon, and I wanted to consume every inch of her. I leaned closer, until our mouths were just a hair's breadth away.

The elevator dinged, signaling our arrival at level twenty three, and I jerked back as the tension shattered. What the hell was I doing? She was here to ruin my reputation, splash my name all over the news as the one who was going to destroy my mother's legacy. Who cared if she smelled like heaven, tasted like sin, and felt better than anything I could remember. Physical attraction did not make up for who she was or what she was here to do.

I stared at the elevator wall as she exited and the doors closed. *Get a freaking grip, man.*

7

Ava

Well, that was probably the least productive interview of my life. I collapsed on my bed and rubbed my temples. Honestly, I had no idea why Kim wanted this interview so bad. I understood the appeal of writing about the transfer in CEO, but who cared about where Arthur grew up and what he'd been doing for the last several years?

Yes, he was rich and taking over a huge business—one of the leading hotel corporations in New York—but there were plenty of more interesting articles to write. Even if we needed to cover this, why interview him? I could get all that information elsewhere, just like I had for the first article.

A sliver of guilt went through me as I remembered his response to that article. It wasn't personal, he had to know that it had nothing to do with him as a person.

Speaking of personal, what the hell was that in the elevator?

One second he was glaring at me like I was leftover gum on his shoe, and the next he was about to kiss me and make me forget my name. Not that I would have let him. No, he was my client, and even if I didn't need to finish a professional interview with him, kissing him or letting him kiss me would have been wrong on so many levels.

Though I was fully aware that we had already done worse, that was before. Before I knew who he was, before he looked at me like I wasn't worth the time of day.

My phone rang and I answered it after the first ring, "Schmidt."

"Ava, how's it going?"

Kim hadn't even left yet, but I wasn't surprised that she was already checking in. If there was a picture next to the word 'micromanaging' in the dictionary, it would be hers.

"It's okay, we were interrupted during our preliminary interview, so I'll have to reschedule that."

"Interrupted by what?"

"I'm not sure, he didn't say. Only that an urgent matter came up."

"I see." A pause. "I don't need to remind you what's riding on this story."

I attempted to keep my voice even as I responded. "No need, I understand the importance of this story." While that might not technically be true, I understood that Kim found it to be of utmost importance.

Another pause before Kim spoke up in a bright voice.

"I want you to schedule a dinner for tonight. I only have a couple hours that I can spare before I leave, but I'll meet you to ensure that some progress is made in regard to this story."

It wasn't a request, and my gut twisted at the thought of trying to interview Art in front of her. I was good at my job, which wasn't prideful, it was just a fact; I worked hard and accomplished my goals, but something about Art threw me off and made me feel completely off-kilter. Maybe it was the fact that I had been naked in bed with him. Whatever it was, I was resolved to overcome it and make this the best interview I had ever completed.

After a few more details, including Kim relaying that she would talk with Arthur's people to make sure they could free up some time for dinner, we ended the call, and I breathed a sigh of relief. I had a couple hours until the dinner she had scheduled, once again micromanaging me. She wasn't a super trusting person, but something about this particular story seemed to affect her differently.

I tried to push that out of my mind as I began another deep dive on Art before dinner.

8

Art

I stepped onto my floor to find Jackson, Cain, and several police officers in my office, none of which were Finn.

"Mr. Michaels," the oldest-looking officer said. He had salt and pepper hair and a goatee.

"I'm officer Sheridan, thank you for agreeing to meet us on such short notice."

"Of course, how can I help you?"

"I understand that you recently took over the CEO position of this hotel."

"That is correct." My stomach knotted. I had a bad feeling that whatever he was about to say was going to throw my already shaky world on its head.

"With that in mind, we wanted to let you know about an ongoing investigation taking place in one of your hotel rooms."

I raised my eyebrows and looked toward Jackson and Cain. This couldn't be good.

"This morning," Sheridan continued, and I looked back

toward him. "One of your guests was found murdered in their bedroom."

My breath caught.

"What?" I asked in disbelief.

"We have officers currently going through the room for evidence, but we were also hoping to use your security cameras."

"Of course, absolutely." I looked toward Jackson. "We have a state of the art security system here, you are welcome to all of it."

Jackson dipped his head in acknowledgment.

"Great. We will use whatever recordings we can and will keep you in the loop about the general progress of the investigation. For now, due to the high profile of the victim, we will be releasing a press statement shortly."

Great. More bad press. Just what I needed. "Do you have any leads or suspicions? Any motive or ideas why?"

"We are not at liberty to say at the moment, but we will let you know when we can."

The officers exited, leaving Jackson, Cain, and I in my office. Cain was uncharacteristically quiet.

"Somebody had to have seen something, right? We have cameras everywhere," I began when we were alone.

Jackson nodded thoughtfully. "Something should be picked up, yes."

I leaned back in my chair and scrubbed my face. "How? Why right now? It really couldn't be more shit timing. And with the *Manhattan Press* already hounding us."

Those words brought a certain blonde-haired brown-eyed girl to mind. This was even more reason for her to stick her nose in everything and write gossip pieces about me and the hotel chain. I groaned again. *Thanks, Mom.*

I really shouldn't be blaming a dead person, but it was hard not to when she got out of all this crap and I was left to stumble through it. For the first time, I started worrying about whether or not I could actually do this.

The night I met Ava, I had gotten a little drunk to try to relieve some of the stress of the impending transition, but up till now, I had never considered the possibility that I couldn't do this. But first, there was the bad press about my ability to handle the responsibility, and now, an incredibly ill-timed murder on my property.

Guilt seeped under my skin. I really should be more concerned about the fact that someone was murdered rather than how it would affect my image, but it had been a rough week.

"I'm sure the detectives will handle it," Cain finally responded, sounding unconvinced and pulling me out of my head.

I glanced at him as he stood. "I should go, put out some fires."

"And I should go help with the security tapes," Jackson replied, rising as well.

They both left my office, and I closed my eyes as I leaned back in my chair. When imagining what life would be like running my mother's company, this had never crossed my mind as a possibility.

I was making plans for my evening that hopefully involved drinking to forget, when Cain popped back into my office.

"Ms. Parly with the *Manhattan Press* just called. She was hoping that we could meet her and Ms. Schmidt tonight for dinner before she leaves. I told her that that should work if it's okay with you."

Dinner with reporters. Exactly how I wanted to spend my evening. Even if one of those reporters happened to be the one dancing through my thoughts on repeat.

"If that's what it takes for them to leave me alone, then I

guess I'll be there."

Cain nodded at me as he exited, and I was again left to my office and my swirling thoughts.

9

Ava

I met Kim in the foyer, and our drive to the restaurant was silent. When we entered, she gave our names and we were taken back to a corner booth, where Art and another man, who I recognized from our first board meeting, sat.

"Kim," the man said as he stood to shake her hand.

"Cain, thank you for making this work on such short notice," she replied with a smile, sliding into the booth.

I sat down next to her and tried to glance casually at the two men, but my attention snagged on Art, and I couldn't look away. He was wearing a plain black t-shirt, which was nothing special, but the way it hugged his muscular arms and the fact that I could see a hint of the tattoo on his bicep beneath his sleeve did weird things to my stomach.

It was completely unfair the way he could look sinful in both a dress shirt and a t-shirt.

My gaze lifted to his face, and I noticed how tired he looked compared to earlier today. What had happened after he had left?

"Ava," Kim's voice pulled me from my wandering thoughts, and I mentally kicked myself. Already not starting out great.

"Yeah, sorry, I appreciate your time, Mr. Michaels."

"Of course, anything I can do to assist you as you write your *thrilling* literature," Art said in a sickly sweet voice. I noticed the disapproving look Cain sent his way.

A waiter came to take our drink orders and deliver bread to the table, which saved me from responding. I tried to regroup. I could do this.

Once they left, I straightened in my chair. "Taking over such a large company before thirty is pretty daunting, and as far as I've been able to tell, you don't have a lot of experience in business."

"Do you have a question or are you simply going to muse about my lack of experience all night?" he asked, taking a drink from his water.

Asshole. I attempted to show my most polite smile, but I could tell it wasn't coming off well.

"You didn't let me finish," I said, attempting, and failing, to keep the edge out of my voice. I heard Kim clear her throat, but I refused to break Art's gaze.

"Well then, by all means, continue on," he said, waving his hand with a flourish.

He wanted to play this game? Fine. I could play.

"What gives you the idea that you are capable of running a multi-million dollar business when the only thing on your resume is attending frat parties?"

I heard a cough and honestly didn't know which direction it had come from, but the room suddenly seemed to have quieted, and Art's cocky grin disappeared. I had obviously struck a nerve.

He leaned forward to place his elbows on the table. "Running a business takes more than a useless, fancy degree.

Not that I would imagine you, as an apprentice, would know, or does your senior journalist always come along to babysit all of the reporters at *Manhattan Press*?"

Anger flooded my veins, and I felt my cheeks heat at the insult. It was true. Kim was here babysitting me because I had been unable to complete the interview on my own, or so she thought. Who was I to be questioning his lack of ability to run the company when I couldn't even complete an interview?

"Service is taking awhile, I think I'll get something from the bar," Kim said as she pushed back. "Ava?"

I was too busy locked in a glaring match with Art to respond, but Cain spoke up from the other side.

"I'll join you."

As soon as they slipped out, the spell holding me in place broke, and I stared down at the uneaten roll on my plate. I heard a loud clatter and looked up just enough to see Art aggressively cutting into his bread as if it were raw steak.

"If I had known you were such a bitch, I wouldn't have gone back to your room," he muttered from his side of the booth. My eyes narrowed.

"Oh, believe me, if I had seen even an ounce of your *charm*, I wouldn't have let you ten feet from me let alone into my bedroom."

"Says the woman who was begging me to fuck her harder and screaming my name so loud the whole hotel heard it."

"Shut the fuck up," I hissed as I looked around us, but no one appeared to be looking our way. "You are a conceited, cocky, asshole."

"Oh, baby, if that's the best you can come up with, you definitely haven't been around me long enough."

Before I could answer, our waiter returned with our drinks, and I seethed as Cain and Kim appeared as well. Somehow I had to get through this dinner without killing him and get enough information to satisfy Kim. At this point, I didn't know which one was going to be harder.

10

Ava

I was still feeling irritated the next morning about letting Art get under my skin like that at dinner. We had finished the meal in a stilted silence, me attempting to ask a question here and there while he did his best not to answer me. Now I had to try to piece together something for an article that would satisfy Kim.

I took a long shower and had just finished drying my hair when my phone buzzed. I inwardly groaned as I answered it.

"Schmidt."

"Ava, I was hoping to chat about your upcoming article," Kim began in a matter of fact tone.

No shit. I figured you were calling to talk about your love life.

"Of course."

We had literally seen each other less than twelve hours ago, I didn't know what she had expected me to have accomplished in the time since we parted ways after dinner. Still, she continued on, and I wondered not for the first time if she even listened to my responses in between her rambling.

"We need to be the first ones to get this out there, you're going to need to talk to the detectives and press them for anything else we can get. I also need you to dig into the guy who died and see if there's anything interesting there."

"Excuse me, what? I'm lost, I thought we were discussing the interview with Arthur."

"Oh my god, catch up. Forget about that, I need you covering this murder."

"What murder?"

Kim let out an exasperated snort, and dread filled me. I didn't know what I'd missed, but it was clearly something important, and incompetence was not something Kim took lightly.

"The murder that literally just took place in the hotel you're staying in, right under your nose?"

A chill ran over me. What had happened? Who died? Was this what Arthur had to deal with when he cancelled the first interview? I braced myself for the incoming tongue lashing I was about to receive.

"I haven't heard about it yet." Where on earth had *she* heard about it?

"Really, Ava, if you weren't already there, I'd pull you from this, but I don't want to waste any time getting this story out there. Someone was murdered in the hotel you're staying at, and I need you to get as much information about it and get it out there before anyone else hears about it."

I refrained from asking where she had gotten this information from or mentioning that until last night, she had also been staying in this hotel. I really didn't feel like losing my job today, and her threat already hung over me.

"Of course, I'll look into it and let you know as soon as I have something."

Kim hung up without another word. Okay, switching gears. Moving on from Arthur.

Despite how huge the hotel was, it shouldn't be too hard to find out which room this took place in. Honestly, it was surprising the story hadn't gotten out yet, as there must have been a pretty big police presence to investigate this. It wasn't like I was staying at a Holiday Inn. Also, what on earth were the chances that someone was murdered while I was here investigating?

I switched into a pair of slacks and a nice blouse before making my way downstairs to the bar, setting up my laptop in the corner. There was only a handful of people here this early, including a couple men and women in business suits and the bartender, who came over to bring me a water.

I set to work scanning my social media, pretending to do something important. Two lemon waters later, and an older woman in a flattering green dress came to sit a couple seats from me. She was on her phone and ordered a cosmopolitan before continuing her phone conversation.

"As I was saying, it was all night long. These rooms are supposed to be the best, but I could still hear them clomping around at all hours."

I kept my eyeroll to myself. There was no way she had been kept awake by someone next door, these rooms might as well have been soundproofed for all the noise you could hear from your room.

"I think it was an overdose."

I tried not to show any reaction to her comment and continued typing away on my computer.

"Well, because I don't think the bastard died from a heart attack." A pause. "Did you know he was cheating on his wife? I think the guilt finally got to him." A laugh. "It could have been the wife, but in that case, I hope she gets away with it."

A man, infidelity, possible suicide? This, I could work with. She moved on to some other topic, and I cleared my throat and leaned toward her, "I'm so sorry to interrupt."

She glanced at me with a mix of annoyance and suspicion.

"I couldn't help but overhear you mentioning the disturbance upstairs. I'm next door too, and the commotion has been incredibly inconvenient. I even had to bring my stuff down here. I'm tempted to file a complaint."

At this, she perked up.

"Hold on, Tammy." She set her phone down. "That's what I was saying! When I booked here, I was expecting better accommodations than all this. Not that they could help it, I suppose, but at least wrap it up sooner."

I nodded, "Exactly. I was going to go talk to the front desk, but I think it might help if I mention that it's not just an isolated incident that's bothering me. Do you mind if I give them your room number as another example?"

"Of course, they should know how inconvenient this whole situation is. I'm in 3603."

"I'll make sure to pass that on when I talk to them."

Seeming satisfied, she went back to her phone conversation, and I wrote down a couple more notes. Floor thirty-six. It was time to get to work.

11

Art

After a morning of confirming details for my mother's funeral, I was on my way to meet with Tanya, the general manager for our New York hotel. I debated between the elevators that I had heard had been experiencing mechanical issues today and the stairs.

Laziness won, and I took my chances with the elevator. When it bypassed my chosen floor and went all the way to the lobby level, I began rethinking my choices. I was just debating getting off and hiking, when the doors opened and Ava entered, staring at her phone, completely oblivious to my presence. My head knew I should be annoyed at her, but tell that to my emotions. Or my dick.

"Oh, sorry, thirty six please—" Her voice trailed off and I cocked an eyebrow.

"I'm pretty sure that's not your floor, unless you've decided to switch rooms in the last thirty six hours."

Her chin rose, and god did I love when she wore that stubborn look. "Am I not allowed to visit other floors now?"

"Touché," I said as I pressed her desired floor and then leaned my shoulder nonchalantly against the wall. And because I couldn't help it I added, "What's so interesting about the thirty-sixth floor?"

"Maybe I made a friend," she said, matching my pose against the other wall. The thought made my stomach clench, but I somehow managed to keep the smirk on my face. "Oh, do tell."

She shrugged as she glanced back down to her phone. "I really don't think it's any of your business."

"Are you always this argumentative?"

"Are you always this nosy?" she shot back.

"I mean, it is *my* hotel, so, yes, I feel entitled to know the *comings* and goings." At this, her gaze finally lifted to meet mine again.

"That sounds highly inappropriate," she said quietly. Her breathy voice brought back images of our first night together. Her perfect naked body, the way she felt around me and moaned my name.

Like a magnet, her eyes sucked me in, and I found myself stepping closer. She attempted to scoot further away from me, but she was already caged in.

I stopped with only inches separating us and reached out to tuck a strand of constantly loose hair behind her ear. It was like she kept it like that just to torture me. Her small intake of breath sent a shot straight to my cock, and my gaze moved down to her mouth.

Her tongue peeked out to wet those perfect lips, and I leaned in close to whisper into her ear, "I have been dreaming of feeling that perfect tongue all over me, little bird."

Her breath shuddered again, and I brushed my lips over the shell of her ear.

She took a deep inhale, and our chests brushed. My cock was already straining against my pants, and I was about to reach down and do something about it, when a shrill scream sounded through the air. She jerked away and I stepped back to spin around. The red alarm on the elevator was blinking, and the sound continued for a moment more before a voice came over the intercom.

"We are sorry for the interruption, this elevator is experiencing a mechanical issue, but it will be resolved shortly."

I glanced at Ava. She had her phone clutched to her chest and a look of frustration on her face. Of all the ways I'd been cock blocked, an elevator alarm was definitely new. But the moment was gone, and she went back to typing furiously on her phone, probably to her boss.

And just like that, I remembered why she was here and why I couldn't stand her.

12

Ava

"Why bird?"

"What?"

Art looked over at me from the floor where he sat, one leg up and his head against the wall. After ten minutes, we had realized it wasn't going to be as quick of a fix as they had made it seem. So, here we were, sitting in silence on opposite ends of the elevator, and no amount of scrolling could take my mind off the feeling of him whispering in my ear, his lips on my skin, the heat in his gaze. Desperate for distraction, I asked the only question I could think of.

"That's twice now that you've called me little bird."

"Ahh." He nodded and ran his hands through his hair. "It's your name."

"What is?"

"I made you forget your name already?" he asked with that infuriating smirk. I glared at him, and he laughed. "Ava. Ava means bird."

"How do you know that? Did you stalk me?"

"Maybe I did."

I wasn't sure how to respond to that. Did I think he stalked me after a one night stand? No. Would I put it past him? Also no.

"It's a weird habit I have," he said with his eyes closed, head resting against the wall.

"Stalking people?"

He peeked an eye open to look at me before settling back in. I didn't think he was going to respond, when he spoke again.

"When I was little, I had a lot of time that I spent by myself. For whatever reason, I've always loved names. I don't really remember how it started, but I began to memorize the meanings of names."

"You just happened to have the meaning of the name Ava memorized?" I asked, incredulously.

He shrugged. "I have a good memory."

"What does Arthur mean?"

"Bear."

"Victoria?"

"That one's kinda cheating because it's pretty self-explanatory. Victorious."

"Leslie."

"Holly garden."

"You're making this up."

He laughed, "Told you, a LOT of time on my hands."

We fell into a surprisingly comfortable silence.

"Who's Leslie?" he asked, finally breaking the silence again.

"Oh, so you didn't stalk me."

He looked back at me with raised brows.

"It's my mom."

"Maybe I said that just to throw you off."

"Oh yeah, so clever."

Another beat of silence.

"Are you close with her?" he questioned.

"I don't know what you consider close, but we see each other every so often for holidays and stuff."

He nodded again.

"Were you close with your mom?" I asked.

The way he'd brushed me off when I brought her up at our first interview could mean several things.

"I hadn't seen her for several months before she passed. When we did see each other, it was mostly for business."

"I'm sorry."

"What for?"

"That just sounds sad."

He shrugged. "The cost of an empire."

"What about your dad?" While I was prying, I might as well continue.

"Never met him. My mom said he was a piece of shit, and that was good enough for me."

Before I could say anything else, the elevator jerked and began moving again. I jumped to my feet and watched it stop at floor thirty six. Honestly, I had forgotten where I had been headed when this all started.

The doors opened, and I looked to see Art still sitting on the floor. Guilt suddenly hit me as I thought about what I was trying to do and the articles I had to write. His eyes were still closed, and I didn't know what else to say, so I left the elevator, the image of Art vulnerable and sad stuck in my brain.

13

Ava

I half expected the floor to be blocked off with police and security, but it looked like any other floor in the hotel.

I attempted to put thoughts of a dark-haired billionaire out of my head, but it was harder than it should have been, and turning on my camera, I checked myself out, running my fingers through my hair and pulling my shirt down a little to expose my cleavage. There weren't a lot of people immune to a good set of boobs. That done, I headed towards 3603.

When I finally rounded the corner, I found a clean-shaven officer standing outside 3605. He had a cute baby face and looked up as I approached. I put on my most charming smile and walked up to him.

"Good morning."

"Good morning," he responded with a smile.

"Busy day today." I nodded at the door behind him. He glanced back at the door and nodded without a word.

"I'm a journalist with the *Manhattan Press* and I was wondering if I could ask you a couple questions."

"Oh," he immediately turned serious. "I'm not supposed to talk to the press."

"Totally," I said as I pulled out a piece of gum from my pocket and popped it into my mouth. Chewing gum worked wonders for presenting an innocent appearance in my experience. "I actually already got the scoop from someone else. I was just curious if I could get some pictures?" I held up my phone.

He laughed, "Yeah, I'm afraid not."

I shrugged as if it didn't matter. "Hey, it was worth a shot, right?"

He relaxed against the door behind him. "Don't know unless you try and all that."

I crossed my arms in what I hoped was a casual gesture but also knew pushed up my boobs. "It's so sad anytime someone dies, but it's especially eerie when it's right in the middle of everybody just living their normal lives."

When he didn't respond, I tried not to grind my teeth in frustration. I was getting nowhere. I tried one last time, "I know there's been multiple other guests who are concerned that something could happen to them too."

He laughed, "Unless you're also a Microsoft exec, I think you'll be fine."

Goldmine. He seemed to realize what he said as soon as it was out of his mouth, but I laughed and popped my gum.

"True. Well, I should get going, but have a nice afternoon."

I waved and headed back to the elevator, taking the car down to my room and setting up my computer again. As the screen came alive, the first thing I saw was an announcement about Laurie Michaels' funeral this afternoon. I immediately texted Kim.

Do you want me at Laurie's funeral today?

No. She responded less than a minute later. I waited for her to send any more information.

The press isn't allowed into the funeral, and there will already been a ton of people covering it from the outside. Keep working on investigating the murder.

I breathed a sigh of relief. I had no interest in running into Art again. Especially on the day of his mother's funeral.

Turning back to the research at hand, I searched Microsoft leadership and found seven top executives, five of them being men. It was a start, but I needed a lot more information to narrow it down. Maybe I could figure out who was in town right now.

I spent the next couple hours searching but ended up no closer to figuring out which executive had been murdered. Kim would just have to be satisfied with the article being more vague than she would like. When the only information I had to go on was that it was a man who may or may not be cheating on his wife, it really didn't help narrow it down.

My phone rang, pulling me out of my internet sleuthing, and I sat back, rubbing at my burning eyes before grabbing my phone to answer it. Vi.

"Hey, babe," I answered with a relieved smile.

"Hey! How long were you planning on being in town before coming to see me?"

I laughed as I leaned back in my chair. "You and what free time?"

"Hey, you know I'll always make time for you. Speaking of which, I have a proposition for you."

"Oooh, you know how I love being propositioned."

Vi laughed and the musical sound floated across the phone.

"You, me, and a new club that just opened here in the city."

"Sounds like a recipe for a disaster."

"Really, A? You avoid me like the bubonic plague, finally come into town, and refuse to even be seen in public with me

—"

"Okay, first off, with that drama, you're sure to win a spot on stage," I said, interrupting her.

She laughed again. "Come on, A, it'll be so fun. Besides, you need to get out, you haven't even been with someone since Chris."

I cringed at the name of my ex and then felt guilt when I thought of Art and how I hadn't told her yet.

"Ava? Why are you so quiet? What are you hiding?"

"Well…"

"Ava Marie Schmidt!"

"It literally happened two days ago, when was I supposed to tell you?"

"Umm, immediately? Yesterday? Today?"

"I'm sorry," I grumbled. "It's been a busy couple of days."

"Okay, so maybe he'll be there tonight."

"Oh no, it was definitely a one-time thing," I said, getting out of my chair and flopping onto the couch.

"Okay, then we'll find you a nice New York boy," she said, undeterred. When I just laughed in response she went on. "Name?"

"What?"

"What was his name? Just so I can make sure that I don't double dip."

"That is disgusting, and his name is Arthur."

"Sounds sophisticated. Was he in his eighties?"

"Victoria, has it ever occurred to you that this is why I didn't tell you?"

She laughed again and shifted the conversation to details for tonight, not sounding the least bit concerned about my complaining. Which was fair, she knew she didn't have anything to worry about. She'd been my best friend since eighth grade, and she knew she was irreplaceable.

I absentmindedly twirled my hair. "I appreciate the break

from work, but I've got to get this article finished if I'm going to meet you tonight."

"Okay, don't work too hard, I can't wait to see you!"

I hung up with a smile. At least something good was coming out of this assignment. It had been too long since I'd made time to hang out with Vi in person. It would be good to see her.

14

Art

My mother's funeral was smaller than I was expecting, given her fame and status. I had left most of the details to other people like Cain, but one of my few requests was that the press be kept out. While I hadn't been extremely close with my mother, I felt it was my obligation to make sure that her funeral not be turned into a spectacle. Everyone deserved some peace in death.

That didn't stop the reporters from camping outside the funeral home, and I purposefully avoided looking to see if Ava was among them.

There would be no viewing of the body, as I had already seen her in the hospital. Instead, she was in a beautiful, closed casket at the front of the room. Whichever one of her staff had picked it had done an excellent job, and I buried the guilt that tried to creep in at the knowledge that I hadn't made those decisions.

The funeral was short, with a priest from the local Catholic church presiding. After the brief service, I stood at the front to greet those who came up to offer their condolences. Most were staff or people who had worked closely with my mom over the years, some were distant family that I vaguely recognized, and many were complete strangers.

I shook hands, accepted flowers, received a few hugs, and finally it was over. She was going to be buried in the same cemetery where her sister had been laid to rest, and a few of us made the drive over for the burial.

I watched them place her into the ground, and a sense of finality hit me. I had known she was dead. I had seen her, talked to the coroner, but until I watched her casket get lowered into the dirt, it hadn't truly sunk in. She was gone, and I was alone in this world. Twenty-seven, more money than I knew what to do with, a company that I wasn't sure I knew how to run, and utterly alone.

I needed a strong drink.

I was tempted to stay in and drink my own stuff, but the idea of sitting with my anxieties all evening pushed me to go to one of the newer clubs that I had been wanting to try, The Crosswalk. Finn had left from the funeral to head to work, so I had to make the trip to the club solo. Probably for the best, considering I wasn't in the mood for conversation.

My driver stopped in front of the three-story building, and I entered with a nod at the bouncer. I was tempted to head straight to the VIP section, but I bypassed the stairs for the bar. The music was blaring a steady beat, and the dance floor was already filled with writhing bodies. I pulled up a seat at the bar and ordered a whiskey sour before I sat back to watch the people around me. Not only was it a nice distraction from my thoughts, but if I happened to find someone to go home with tonight, that would make it even better.

I was taking another sip of my drink when my phone buzzed. Jackson. *You might want to check this out.* I clicked on the link he sent and immediately wished I hadn't. It brought me to a news article posted by none other than Ava freaking Schmidt.

Man found dead in luxury Laurie hotel

On Saturday evening, an executive for Microsoft was found murdered in his hotel room. The NYC police department declined to comment on any possible cause of death or suspects, but according to other guests at the hotel, there are concerns for overdose or even foul play. "I don't know what's going on, but the police have been in and out of that room for hours, definitely not the relaxing stay I was planning," said one guest with a room near that of the deceased.

The article went one with no real new information, but I had read enough. Cue the media storm. I rubbed my forehead. I knew it was bound to come out, and it wasn't fair to direct all of my frustration at Ava, but how had she gotten wind of it so fast? She was starting to become a major pain in my ass. Every time her name appeared, drama followed.

I swallowed the rest of my drink and texted him back. *Read it. Anything so far?*

News stations already outside the hotel, Came his response.

Of course. I gritted my teeth and pocketed my phone, nothing else to say to that.

After waving at the bartender for another, I turned back to scan the room while I waited. A flash of red caught my eye, and I honed in on the sight as a thrill of adrenaline went through me. Curvy ass, backless, short, red dress, and blonde hair pulled back into clips that I very much wanted to run my fingers through.

She turned, and I swore under my breath. The universe was truly punishing me for something, because, really? Ava freaking Schmidt.

She must have felt me staring, because she turned from the woman she was with, and our gazes locked. Speak of the devil.

Her friend must not have noticed the current running between us, because she grabbed her by the hand and dragged her to the bar and the open spot right next to me. She was oblivious, waiting for the bartender. I nodded at Ava.

"Ava."

"Arthur."

I couldn't help my raised brow. "Oh, so it's Arthur now?"

"That is your name, isn't it?"

I propped my chin on my hand, "It wasn't Saturday night."

What was I doing? This was the villainous reporter trying to sabotage my job.

I blamed the dress. Last time, I could blame the alcohol, but right now, I was currently only on drink number one. No, it must be the dress. The way it hugged her curves in all the right spots. Fuck, she was delicious.

A blush stained her cheeks, and the sight made my cock harden. She then raised a brow. "Oh, so we're pretending like that happened now?"

"What do you mean pretending?"

"I mean how the next day you pretended we had never met and you couldn't give me the time of day."

"Oh, you mean like when you came into my hotel to criticize my business even further? Or the time you wrote an article about how *unrelaxing* my accommodations are?"

She had the decency to look slightly guilty, but it only lasted for a second. "I'm sorry that me doing my job angers you. Believe me, as soon as I can, I will get out of your life."

"Good."

"Sorry to interrupt," a female voice said with a slight cough, "I'm Victoria."

I finally tore my gaze from Ava to take in the tall, olive-skinned brunette next to her.

"Art," I said, glancing back at Ava.

"How do you know each other?"

"This is Arthur Michaels."

Victoria's mouth opened into a large 'O.' "You're him."

I let out a laugh, but before I had a chance to question her further, Ava grabbed her hand and pulled her toward the dance floor. "Come on, you owe me a dance."

Victoria reluctantly let her friend pull her away, and I watched in amusement, which quickly turned to something else as I sipped my drink. The friends danced, laughed, and I swear Ava purposefully shook her ass in my direction.

Someone came up to me and said something, but I responded with a noncommittal answer while my gaze stayed glued to the girls. I didn't know what it was about her that intoxicated me, but it did, It felt like being near her was the equivalent of downing a six pack. This evening was turning into the opposite of relaxing.

15

Ava

"So, you want to tell me about it?" Vi asked with a raised brow as we swayed to the music.

"About what?" I attempted my most innocent look.

"Umm, the dark and broody man in the corner who won't take his eyes off of you and is definitely not in his eighties."

I followed her gaze to where Art was indeed staring at me from his spot at the bar.

"There's nothing to tell."

"Oh yeah, cause it's normal for your one night stand to look like he wants to strangle you and fuck you at the same time."

I was about to argue but she had a point. "You know, they say there's a fine line between hate and lust."

She laughed. "Was the sex really that bad?"

"No," I answered a little too quickly, eliciting a grin from my bestie. I sighed. "You know I'm here for an article, well he's the one I'm writing the article about."

Her eyes grew huge. "So, your interview turned into a

hookup?"

"No! We slept together before I knew he was the one I was here to interview," I said, cringing. "And to make matters worse, he kind of owns the hotel I'm staying at."

If I thought her eyes were huge before, they turned into saucers at my admission.

"Oh, my, God. He must be loaded."

I laughed. "Yeah, and he was excellent in bed; however, he hates my guts for writing about him."

"Damn, his loss," she said with a shrug.

"His loss? Did you not just hear what I said?"

"Yes, but have you seen yourself? Who cares about money when he could have you."

"You're ridiculous," I said with a laugh.

"Maybe," she said as the music changed and we continued to dance.

# # #

An hour later, we were thoroughly sore, drunk, and happy. When Vi had first invited me out, I had been extremely tempted to hole myself up in my room and continue researching. But I had gotten the article out, contacted Kim to let her know how it was going, and I deserved some fun, dammit. And now I was so glad that I had.

Vi and I used the bathroom before we stumbled outside and hugged each other goodbye. My hotel was in the opposite direction of her apartment, so it didn't make sense to split an uber. I pulled up the app on my phone, when I heard a deep voice in front of me.

"Get in the car." My heart plummeted right to my gut, but I was standing next to the patio, so there was no way someone was trying to kidnap me right next to a crowd. I looked up to find Arthur staring at me.

"Excuse me?"

"We're heading back to the same place. My driver is here," he said in a clipped voice, motioning to the car in front of us. "Get in the car."

"What if I don't feel like sharing a ride with you?" I said, tossing my hair back.

"Get. In. The. Car," he ground out.

The command in his voice sent a rush through me, and my limbs moved without my permission as he held the door open and I slid in. He got in after me, and as soon as the door closed, we were moving.

"What's with your face?" I asked, a little more breathlessly than I intended.

"You."

"Me? What did I do?"

"Nothing. Everything. You wore that fucking dress and shook your ass all night."

"I did not!" Okay, maybe I did. Maybe I had noticed the heat in his gaze and thought it would be fun to put on a little show. But my dress wasn't *that* crazy.

"Really?" he said as he leaned toward me. I scooted toward the end of the bench, and he followed right behind me. "Ava."

"Yes," I breathed, smelling the whiskey on his breath.

"You really shouldn't have gotten into my car if you wanted to stay away from me."

I didn't have time to respond before his lips were on mine. He was kissing, consuming me. He sucked my lip between his teeth, and I gasped at the sensation. My hands involuntarily slid into his hair and tugged at his roots. He groaned, pulling back just the slightest bit.

"You have no idea what you do to me. I can't get you out of my head. Your smell, feel, taste," he said again before plunging back into my mouth. I moaned into him, arching my back to meet his body. He reached down and hiked my dress up, allowing me to wrap my legs around his waist. He wasn't lying, I really did do something to him. Something very hard and very thick that pressed into me exactly where I wanted him. After the last several days of doing my best to keep him at arm's length, my body was strung so tight that the slightest touch threatened to make me implode.

His hand slid up my neck to grab my hair, pulling at the pins. I gasped at the slight pain in my scalp followed by a rush of pleasure as he gripped my hair and crushed me to him.

Then suddenly he was pulling away, making me feel incredibly empty and cold. I watched with hooded eyes as he reached forward, lifted me by my hips, and slid himself under me. I gasped as he set me back down on him, his hot breath fanning across my center. Even through my underwear, the sensation was too much and not enough at the same time.

"Arthur," I whimpered.

He pulled back. "Absolutely not."

"What?" I breathed in my lust-fueled haze.

"That is not what you call me if you want something. And you do want something, don't you?" He slid his finger along my thong, pulling it to the side before pressing a soft kiss to my vagina. I groaned and attempted to ride his face, but his grip on my hips tightened, keeping me away from where I wanted to be.

I glared down at him as I attempted harder to fight him, but my hips went nowhere in his punishing grip.

"What do you say when you want something?" He finished his question with another kiss, and I moaned again. I needed friction, anything.

"Please."

"Please what, little bird?

"Please eat me out, let me ride your face," I gasped as I attempted to buck against him again. This time he let me go, plunging his tongue straight into me. I arched my back with a cry, "Art!"

"Yes, little bird?" he mumbled against me, and I couldn't even formulate a response as I rode his face and he devoured my pussy. The sensation was the greatest thing I'd felt in my life. I simultaneously wanted this to last forever and also desperately needed to finish. I felt an orgasm building in my core, but just before I found release, he pulled back again.

"What the fuck!" I demanded as he smirked.

"You really need to be more specific, love. You asked to ride my face, did you not just ride my face? Did I not just eat you out?"

I glared down at him, "Yes, but—"

"Specific, love, what do you want?" he said as he made a slow lick up my center and pressed his thumb to my clit.

"Fuck! Let me cum, please. Please," I begged louder as he teased my clit with his tongue once more.

"Of course. Why didn't you just ask me?"

I wanted to smack him, but between his mouth and his fingers, I was a bomb that was exploding after being set for far too long, and I came on a loud cry as he pressed kiss after kiss to my center until I was spent.

While I slumped against him, he slid up from under me to brush my hair from my face and press a kiss to my mouth. I tasted myself on him and almost moaned again until I realized that we were no longer moving. I sat up with a start.

"Where are we?"

"It appears we have arrived back at the hotel."

I scrambled off of him, pulling my dress down. "Has your driver just been sitting in the front the whole time?" I accused.

He laughed as he smoothed down his shirt. "Alanzo? No,

he knows to just leave if I'm not ready when we park."

"Oh." I tried to pull together my frazzled thoughts. "Well, I'm glad you guys have a nice system down."

"Are you jealous, love?" he said with an infuriating smirk on his face, his arm propped against the back seat as if he had all the time in the world.

"Of course not, and stop calling me that."

His smirk expanded into a full-blown smile. "Of course."

I scooted to the door and pushed it open without a look back.

"Do you know where you're going?" he asked from behind me.

"I'll figure it out," I said without a backward glance. His answering chuckle followed me as I marched as fast as my heels would take me to the nearest elevator.

16

Art

That had been a mistake. I knew it before I even opened my mouth, but I couldn't help it. I had been strung tight all night, watching her was the sweetest torture, and when she happened to stop right next to my car as I was leaving, it was like fate shoved her into my lap. Or onto my face.

I cursed at the slowness of the elevator, and when it finally reached my floor, I walked straight to the bathroom, stripping before stepping into the lukewarm water. The look on her face as she had realized where we were and what we had done was priceless. Yet I was the one who was supposed to be avoiding her.

She had no reason to dislike me, I'd done nothing wrong. She was the one who came in like a hurricane, upsetting my already scattered life and sending me chasing after her like a teenage boy with his first crush.

I let the cold water rush over me in hopes that it would calm my raging boner, but it did nothing to cool the lust pouring through my veins. The memory of her gasping my name, staring down at me, begging me, consumed my mind.

I groaned as I fisted my cock and began pumping in time to the images in my head. I imagined it was her hand wrapped around my shaft instead of mine, slowly stroking me up and down. My breath came in pants as I felt tension coil at the base of my spine. I imagined her pressed against the shower wall as I pounded into her and she screamed, begging me for more.

My cock throbbed and my balls begged for release. There was no sweeter sound than her begging me to fuck her harder, to eat her out until her pussy exploded. She could ask me anything in that moment and I would oblige.

In an embarrassingly short amount of time, I was coming so hard I saw stars. I stood gasping under the stream of water as disgust at myself filled me. I really needed to go out and find someone else to replace the memory of her.

17

Murderer

I had been tempted to flip a coin to pick my next kill. I had plenty of options to choose from but nothing particularly against any of those currently staying at the Laurie. Probably for the best, as I didn't want this to get personal or come back to me. So far, I had the investigators and security teams running in circles. This next murder would probably change that, but I knew I was covering my tracks well.

I glanced down at my device to triple check that the security cameras in this part of the hotel were being occupied. Satisfied, I placed the bottle of wine on my tray and approached the door. I knocked and, after a few moments, it was opened by a middle-aged woman with dark skin that sagged despite her plastic surgery.

"A complimentary bottle of wine from Mr. Michaels."

"Oh," she stepped back to let me in like I had predicted she would. I walked the wine over to her kitchenette.

"That is so kind of him. Was there a particular reason he sent it over?"

I placed the bottle on the counter and adjusted my white gloves to make sure that they were firmly in place before turning back to the woman before me. She had a quizzical expression on her face as she waited for my answer. It shouldn't come as a surprise to me that she believed the owner of the hotel where she was staying had sent her free wine or even knew she was here. They were all the same. Arrogant.

I reached into my pocket, pulling out a wire. Her gaze followed my movement, but before she had a chance to say anything I had it wrapped around her throat as I pulled her to my chest, holding tight. She struggled and squeaked out what air she had left, leaving her without any breath.

She continued to claw at my shirt sleeves, but I held on tight. Despite her age and small stature, her adrenaline gave her an extra boost of strength that made my arms ache in response. Finally, she stilled, and I held on a moment longer before gently setting her on the floor. I didn't need any unnecessary loud noises causing alarm.

Once she was on the floor I dropped the wire that I had used on top of her and gave the room a quick sweep to make sure that I hadn't dropped anything. Satisfied, I adjusted my gloves again and opened my phone to check the cameras outside the room. The hallway was empty, and I made sure the security video was still looping.

I left the room, making sure the do not disturb sign wasn't on the handle. I needed the maids to find her sooner rather than later. Soon that spoiled brat would realize how incompetent he was at running this hotel, and he would watch his life come crashing down around him like I had.

Sneaking into the security room was easier than expected. It was late and the security guard in the tech room was clearly not expecting someone to come by. When I told him that I needed to check out the cameras for Arthur, he let me in without an issue. He went back to his desk, and I found a spot far enough away that he would have to come stand over my shoulder to see what I was doing.

I logged in with Arthur's credentials and found the file that I was looking for. A quick check over my shoulder let me know that the guard was engrossed with something on his phone. Several keystrokes later, and I had replaced the footage that I'd removed with a section from earlier that night. It wasn't seamless, and if someone went looking, they would easily see the splice. That wasn't my concern. As long as there was no evidence of me entering her room, that was all I needed.

I had taken my time to learn the ins and outs of the security program that Arthur used, and I knew enough to feel confident that they had no proof that I had even been on that floor tonight.

With a couple more taps, I logged out and nodded to the guard.

"All good."

"Oh, good. Have a good night."

I left without another word. I was taking a chance coming here and not killing the guard, but I'd taken precautions with my appearance, and if he were grilled about who came by today, the description of a bald man with a beard wouldn't lead back to me. Sabotaging Arthur was turning into quite the ordeal, but it would all be worth it in the end when I got to witness his empire come crashing down around him.

18

"So, you've forgiven her?"

I grunted as I blocked a punch from Finn and returned one of my own. "Do I appreciate her writing trash articles about me and the company? No. Do I appreciate the way her body feels under mine? Quite possibly."

Finn halted, holding up his hand "Whoa, whoa, too much information."

I took the opportunity to take another swing at him, "I wasn't going to tell you anything else, asshole. Plus, it was a mistake and it won't happen again."

"I'm pretty sure that's what you said last time."

I glared at him. "Watch it."

He smirked as he stepped back, taking a swig from his water bottle. "Well, if she's grown on you, maybe you should invite her to the gala."

I groaned. "Please don't remind me of that."

"It was your mom's favorite charity, you have to go; otherwise, Ava won't be the only one writing unflattering pieces on you."

He had a point. I really had no choice but to go. But that didn't mean I had to bring anyone with me. Especially Ava.

An image of her in a skintight dress, hugging my side all night flitted through my brain. It might not be that terrible. If only I could separate her body from her personality.

My phone buzzed from the chair behind me, and I stepped back to check who it was. Jackson. I was getting really sick of seeing that name come across my messages. *Need you back here immediately.*

"What now?" I muttered.

"What's that?"

"I gotta head back and deal with whatever emergency has popped up now. A week in, and I already hate this job. You wanna catch a ride?"

"Yeah, sure, always happy to take advantage of your luxury."

I rolled my eyes. "Okay, mooch."

We gathered our stuff and headed to my car. Some traffic later, and we pulled into my underground parking spot. I tried to forget how I arrived here the last time, but a smirk crossed my face remembering Ava's shock when she realized we had stopped without her noticing.

"Something you wanna share with the class?"

"Not a chance," I said as I pushed his shoulder and we headed upstairs.

"Hey, I want to stop by and get a beer that I can actually stomach, unlike the crap you have in your room."

"Liar, the only reason you want to stop here is to see if that bartender you like is working."

"What, me? You wound me," he said, clutching his chest.

She was in fact not working today, but he stayed to grab his drink anyway, and I waited for him as an excuse to delay whatever bad news Jackson had for me.

"Excuse me, but I couldn't help but notice what an exquisite necklace that is," I heard from my side. I rolled my eyes as I turned to see who had caught his eye this time. My best friend was a notorious womanizer, and something about his red curls and slight Irish accent worked almost every time.

My blood went cold and then hot when I saw the blonde hair.

"Arthur." I saw my surprise reflected back in her gaze.

"Ava."

"Ava? *The* Ava?" Finn said almost giddily as he looked between us.

I was going to punch him and revoke his penthouse privileges.

To Ava's credit, she looked at him suspiciously, and he quickly stuck out his hand with a lopsided grin.

"Sorry, I'm Finn, Art's told me all about you."

She turned her suspicious gaze to me but shook his hand anyway. Screw punching, I was going to go straight to removing his tongue.

She seemed to gather herself, putting on a fake smile. "Well, it's nice to meet you Finn. Do you work here too?"

He let out a boisterous laugh. "Absolutely not, no amount of money in the world could pay me to work for Art. I've known him since boarding school."

That was enough. I could see the glint in her eyes as she got ready to pull some more dirt from him for her ridiculous articles.

"Jackson's waiting," I told Finn stiffly.

He looked at me like he couldn't believe I was cutting this short. "Well, it was nice to meet you," he said, giving her a friendly smile.

Either it was his magic charm, or she really was plotting how to use him, but she gave him a bigger, more authentic smile this time. "You, too."

I turned to go, but Finn spoke up again. "Oh, I almost forgot to ask, are you going to the gala tomorrow night?"

"What gala?" Ava asked.

I was methodically moving on to evisceration.

"The fundraiser for leukemia that Laurie hosts every year. Art told me he was going to ask you to come as his plus one."

There went his liver.

I turned back to see a frown wrinkle her forehead. "Oh, well, no, I'm not planning on it."

"Oh, come on, you have to! If you're here to write a story on Art and the Laurie, the gala could prove very beneficial for you."

Spleen.

She turned her gaze to me, and I finally conceded. "It's over at the Ramada, seven o'clock."

She nodded, and Finn stepped in one last time, "There's plenty of space for you in his car, we'll drive together."

Her cheeks pinked at his unintentional reference to my car, and I took that as my exit.

"We'll meet you in the lobby, six thirty. If you'll excuse me."

I walked toward the elevator, afraid of leaving Finn alone with her but equally disturbed at the prospect of standing making small talk for another second. In the heat of the moment, like last night, I couldn't care less about her job and why she was here, but something about seeing her in my hotel brought all of that back centerstage and sent a flame of irritation through me.

"Thanks so much for that," I growled at Finn once we were in the elevator heading up.

"Dude, you did *not* do her justice," he said as he whistled. The sound grated on my nerves, and I balled my hands into fists.

"Speak like that about her again and you'll lose your ability to use your tongue."

He took a step back and threw his hands up in the air. "Sorry, sorry, my bad."

The rest of the ride was taken in silence, and we finally stepped onto my floor. Angie motioned to my office, and all thoughts of Ava fled as I entered to see Jackson, Cain, and several detectives.

What could it possibly be now? Maybe they had news on the cause of death. Maybe they had someone in custody.

"Mr. Micheals, I'm sorry to keep meeting like this," said the gray-haired detective from before. Sheridan, if I remembered correctly.

"Is there an update on the case?" I asked as I slid behind my desk across from them. The detectives glanced at Finn, and I waved my hand for them to continue as he leaned against the wall behind me.

"Sort of. There's been another murder."

Another murder? This was New York, people were murdered all the time. Maybe it was the same MO and they had a serial killer on their hands?

"Where at?"

"Here." The air punched out of my lungs.

"Here?" I echoed in disbelief.

Sheridan nodded as he rubbed his chin. "Different room, doesn't seem to be any connection to the first murder. The only link is this hotel."

My hotel. I had a serial killer using my hotel as their hunting grounds?

I felt a familiar rage course through me and tried to keep the darkness at bay, but I could feel that thing crawling beneath my skin. A need for vengeance, to right the wrong.

From a young age, I'd experienced this all-consuming drive that had started in small ways when a classmate pushed a little too hard, talked a little too much. It had morphed over the years, the last occurrence being my response to the dealer who wanted to take advantage of my mother's wealth. And now I felt that same response; however, this time I had nowhere to aim my anger.

"Something had to have been caught on the security tapes," I insisted, looking towards Jackson. His normally dark skin was a shade paler, and he looked like he might be sick.

"No, sir, the tapes appear to have been tampered with, we weren't able to get anything of value off of them." Shit. Tampered with?

"Who has access to the security system?" I grilled Jackson.

Sheridan stepped in again, "We are working hard to try to answer all those questions, and we will find whoever is doing this, but we just wanted you to be prepared."

"Prepared for what? That my guests are just going to keep dropping left and right?" I snapped.

"I assure you, we are doing everything we can to catch who's responsible for this, and we are taking every precaution and security measure to keep the guests here safe. So far, this information has not leaked, but when it does…"

He didn't need to finish that sentence. It was one thing to stay in a hotel where someone had been murdered. But two murders? In a week? I wouldn't blame the public for erecting a barbed wire fence around this place to keep themselves safe, but what the hell was I going to do?

There had already been such bad press. Laurie had done well for the company, and business was thriving, but there were only so many hits it could take at one time and remain standing.

"One last thing," Sheridan said, pulling me from my thoughts. "We are going to need you to come down to the station to answer some questions."

"Am I a suspect?"

"No, we simply have some routine questions."

I looked at Finn, and if I hadn't already known that I needed a lawyer, his facial expression confirmed it.

Despite my illegal activities over the years, I'd never actually been interrogated or arrested. I had never imagined that the first time would happen over something that I actually had nothing to do with.

"I will have my lawyer contact you," I said, turning back to face them.

Sheridan took that as well as he could, and the detectives saw themselves out, leaving me to face Cain and Jackson.

"They might think they have this under control, but they're clearly not doing enough, so I want every resource focused on this. Redo background checks, limit who has access, fire everyone and start new if we have to."

Jackson nodded at my list of demands.

"Do you have any idea how the system is being tampered with?" I asked him.

"Not to interrupt, but I think you have more pressing matters," Cain spoke from the other side of the desk.

"More pressing than a murderer loose in my hotel?" I questioned with a raised brow.

"Yes, well, leave that to the experts. In other news, we've also had several large investors threatening to pull their support."

"Why is this the first time I'm hearing about this?"

"I have been in communication with them so far, your mother—"

"I am not my mother."

Cain's jaw clenched and he bit out, "My point is, if we don't do something soon, I'm afraid more are going to follow suit. Especially with this new development."

Cain was a dick. But he was right. I needed to do something.

"Call a meeting with the investors. I also want to talk with Ruby and Nathan about all of this. Get something set up," I said to Cain before turning toward Finn, effectively dismissing my COO. "Can I skip the gala now?"

He winced as he shook his head. "Now is even more of a reason for you to go woo the public."

I groaned but knew he was right. That didn't mean I had to like it.

I turned to Jackson, who remained in the room, looking over something on his phone. "I'd like to see the security tapes, not that I don't trust you to do your job, but still."

He dipped his head. "We can go down there now if you'd like."

I nodded and followed Jackson downstairs to the security room. I'd been in here before but not frequently. The room contained a wall of monitors and one-way glass that allowed us to see into the lobby. Several people sat in front of the computers with headsets on, but they glanced up and acknowledged us with nods as we entered. On the other side of the room was a door that led to Jackson's personal office, and we entered, closing the door behind us.

He sat down and, after entering his security information, a stream pulled up. "After the first murder, we doubled the security presence so that we had extra eyes on all of the floors. We have at least one camera on each floor by the elevator and stairwells so we can see who enters and exits. We obviously have no cameras inside the guest rooms, as that is a privacy violation."

I watched as he pulled up the feed for the fifty-second floor. "Time of death appears to be roughly eight p.m., so we went back to five o'clock to rewatch. It's unclear exactly when it happens, but sometime before eight, the tapes begin to loop and the security footage from that time was deleted."

"How?"

"We're still working on that part," he answered with a wince.

"There isn't a way to trace who tampered with it?"

"Unfortunately, before now, we didn't have any program to track that, no."

"What about after the first murder?"

"They were still trying to figure out exactly what happened yesterday, so, no, nothing was put into place."

"That's unacceptable," I bit out.

"I know," Jackson said solemnly. "I take full responsibility. We have now added security measures so that if someone attempts to tamper with it again, I will not only be alerted but it requires multiple authentication steps to even get into the program."

I wanted to cuss him out over his lack of security measures prior to this, but what was done was done. There was nothing we could do now except make sure that it couldn't happen again.

"I want to know the minute something weird comes back. I also want to know who was on security during those two days and I want them removed."

"I already have a list of those working, and it was different people each time. I'll make sure that their access is revoked until we get this figured out."

There was nothing more I could do at the moment, so I left him in his office and headed back to my room, sending a message to my lawyer as I did.

<h1 style="text-align:center">19</h1>

Ava

I had woken up this morning still seething from the night before, and then, just my luck, I ran into Art and his friend downstairs. What was his problem? The last time I saw him, he was smirking after giving me one of the best orgasms of my life. Then twelve hours later, he was as cold and aloof as he'd been in the boardroom. Not that I minded. I would rather a cold Arthur who despised the ground I walked on to the one who looked at me with such heat that I couldn't think about anything but getting closer to him.

I shook my head. Bad Ava. The first time, I hadn't known who he was, the second time had been a slip-up. It would not happen a third.

My first instinct was to say absolutely no to this gala, but spending time with him would help in getting more information out of him. Despite the murder and Kim's desire to have me switch gears to that, she had still been hounding me about finding more dirt to pull up on Arthur.

So far, I hadn't found anything new that hadn't already

been splashed all over the front page. I needed something else to work with, and, even though he hadn't appeared thrilled to bring me, Finn hadn't given him much choice. Even from the short interaction I'd had with him, Finn seemed fun, and I had no doubt I could get him to tell me more about his friend.

Thinking about the upcoming articles sent anxiety pouring through me, so instead I moved on to my wardrobe.

Because I hadn't packed anything suitable for an expensive gala, I needed an emergency shopping run. Thankfully, Vi was free after her shift at the club she waitressed at, and we met downtown in the shopping district. She pulled me into a hug when I met her inside.

"You know how long it's been since we've been shopping properly? I'm so excited to make you buy things!"

I laughed at her enthusiasm. "Yes, it has been awhile, but we're sticking to a budget here, I don't have endless funds to spend on this shopping spree."

"Can't you write it off as a work related expense?"

I gave her a mock glare. "Somehow, I don't see Kim agreeing that an evening gown is good use of company resources."

"But it *is* for work," Vi argued as she examined the first rack of dresses.

"True, but I could just as easily interview him without attending this gala."

"So then, why *are* you going? Not that I blame you, I'm extremely jealous of you drinking champagne and mingling with all of those rich people."

"Come with me! I really don't want to go alone."

"I wasn't invited." She lifted up her hand when I tried to protest. "Plus, I am finally getting a chance to meet Winnie. Nothing is going to get in the way of that opportunity."

She had a point. I knew how excited she was to meet

Winnie, and I would never jeopardize an opportunity for her, even if that meant sacrificing my comfort.

Vi had moved to New York with the sole purpose of auditioning for the New York City Ballet. So far, she'd had no luck, so she waitressed while networking. But now, her hard work was paying off because she had finally gotten a chance to meet one of the directors. It wasn't an audition, but it was a start.

"You know how proud I am of you?" I looped my arm through hers and gave it a squeeze. "My best friend, going to be starring in the Nutcracker before we know it."

She laughed as her cheeks turned pink.

"Let's not get ahead of ourselves. Now, come on! We don't have much time, and we have to find you something perfect. "

After some trial and error, we settled on a floor-length red gown with bejeweled straps and a slit up the thigh. According to Vi, it was "breathtaking and perfect for the gala, sure to make every man's heart stop." She was always dramatic, but that was one of the many reasons why I loved her.

We parted with another long hug, and I felt a pang at the thought of going back to my condo once this article was done. I loved all of the hustle and bustle of the city, and the ability to call up Vi at any moment to meet up was amazing. Plus, when she did get a position at the ballet, I wanted to be close for that. But it wasn't like I could just up and relocate permanently for work.

I sighed as I took a cab back to the hotel. Those were concerns for another day. At the moment, I needed to come up with my game plan on how to get more information out of Arthur.

20

Art

After contacting my lawyer, Lacy, we both met at the police station. She was a middle-aged woman with sharp angles and a no-nonsense expression permanently stamped on her face.

"Arthur," she said as we were directed to an office room.

"Lacy," I responded back.

When she was satisfied that we were alone, she pulled out her notebook. "Anything that I need to know?"

"Nothing. I'm as shocked as everyone else about this."

"Do you have an alibi for Saturday or Monday?"

"Both," I responded, pulling up Ava's contact information. I hoped that her dislike of me wouldn't cause any issues when someone contacted her to ask if we truly had been together, then dismissed the thought. I knew she didn't like me, but she would never lie about our whereabouts to incriminate me.

Detective Sheridan and another officer entered several moments later.

"Thank you for coming in," Sheridan said, obviously

taking point on the investigation.

"What can we do for you?" Lacy asked.

"We're just covering our bases here. Is it correct that you officially took over the company as CEO?"

I looked toward Lacy, and when she nodded, I answered, "That is correct."

"And the first murder occurred a day later."

"Are you asking us to confirm the date of the murder?" Lacy asked.

"No, I was simply mentioning the fact."

I stayed silent. I'd received enough legal advice to know not to speak unless Lacy expressly told me to.

"Is it also correct that your mother died of suspicious causes?" he asked next.

"What does this have to do with the current murders?" Lacy questioned.

"I'm just trying to put the whole picture together."

"I don't believe that has anything to do with this current case. Is my client under investigation for that too?"

"No, we are simply trying to gather all of the information."

After another nod from Lacy, I responded. "As far as I know, the cause of her death was ruled as an accident due to Botox poisoning. I'm unaware if that company is under investigation or not."

"Kind of weird that your mother passed unexpectedly, you took over the company, and now we've had another two suspicious deaths, don't you think?"

"Do you have an actual question or are you attempting to interrogate my client on his feelings around his mother's death?"

Sheridan cleared his throat and looked down at his legal pad. "Where were you Saturday evening?"

"I was at the hotel, I went down to the bar, spent some time in a friend's room, and then went back to my suite."

"Can anyone confirm that?"

"Yes. You should be able to see on the security cameras as well as talk to the bartender and the woman that I was with."

"And Monday?"

"I was at The Crosswalk until around midnight. You can talk to my driver Alanzo."

He nodded as he scribbled down some notes.

"Is that all?" Lacy asked after a moment of silence.

"Yes, I believe that is all for now. We will be in touch."

"Of course," Lacy said, and I stood with her to exit.

"Should I be concerned?" I asked as we left the building.

"No, there should be more than enough evidence to prove you weren't anywhere near the crimes scenes during those times."

"Thank you for coming."

"Call me if you hear anything else," she said as we parted ways.

I slid behind the wheel of my car and leaned my head against the seat with a sigh. I trusted Lacy, and if she thought I would be fine, I believed her. I knew I had nothing to do with the murders, but that didn't make being interrogated any easier. And now I had to go try to convince some of our biggest investors not to pull their funds. This wasn't at all what I had imagined for my first week as CEO.

I really needed to schedule some more time at the shooting range or boxing with Finn to release some of this tension that I couldn't seem to get rid of no matter how much I tried.

21

Ava

My phone rang as I was finishing getting ready for the day, and I blinked in surprise when my mom's picture popped up on the screen.

"Hey, Mom."

"Hello, honey, how are you?"

"I'm doing okay," I said, already bracing for her reason for calling. She didn't ever just call for small talk.

"That's good, that's good." A moment of silence. "I was just calling because I ran into Lydia's mom the other day. You remember Lydia from school, right?"

How could I forget? My mom had only been obsessed with her my whole life. "Yep, I remember Lydia."

"Good, I was just talking to her mom, and she told me that she just got this big promotion at her company last month."

I put my mom on speakerphone as I continued applying mascara. "Mhm," I responded.

"Yeah and she had asked about you, and I said you were still working at that news company."

I tried to keep my frustration at bay. Even after all these years, she'd refused to remember the name of the company where I worked.

"Yep," I responded again.

"Well, I mentioned how you haven't really been making any progress, and she said that she bet Lydia could put in a good word for you."

I set the mascara down at the rush of anger that enveloped me. "Mom, Lydia works for a grocery chain, I'm in journalism—"

"Oh, don't worry. I asked her about the qualifications for a front desk job at her company, and she said it only requires an associate's degree."

"Mom," I said, firmer, interrupting her, "I don't want or need a secretarial position."

"Oh, don't be ridiculous, Ava, you've been working at that newspaper for years now without anything to show for it. Lydia is in upper management, I'm sure with her recommendation, she could help your career advance."

"I have to go. I actually have a gala that I have to attend tonight for my current job as a journalist."

"Okay, but this offer probably won't be available for long. Once you get done with whatever you're doing, I would highly suggest you reach out to Lydia. You have her number, right?"

"Yep," I said through gritted teeth. "Okay, I gotta go, bye."

I hung up and closed my eyes against the emotions warring inside me. She had never been happy about my choice to pursue journalism. From the very beginning, she had tried to convince me to take a different path. Yet I still clung to the hope that one day, she would realize that this was what I wanted and stop trying to push me in other directions. Apparently not.

My eyes burned as I forced the emotion back. I would not

cry over this again. The worst part was I didn't even think she was doing it maliciously. She was just so self-absorbed, so unaware of me and what I actually wanted, it was as if she didn't even hear me when I argued or asked her to stop pushing. It shouldn't affect me like this anymore, I wasn't a child. But at this point, I might never outgrow my desire for her validation and pride for me.

I attempted to put the conversation out of my mind as I reapplied my mascara and finished my makeup. Normally, I would just order room service, but after that call, I wanted to be around people and out of my own thoughts, even if only for a little while.

I grabbed my computer bag and headed for the dining area. I'd heard good things about the breakfast here but hadn't yet tried it besides the few dishes I'd ordered to my room.

I reached the dining area to the sound of silverware clanking and people chatting and went through the buffet line, picking my omelet ingredients and finding a corner booth to sit at while I worked. I had just opened my computer, when I heard a familiar voice.

"Ava!"

I looked up to meet Finn's green gaze. He slid into my booth without asking, and I was about to respond, when I saw Art glaring from where he stood behind Finn. "I thought we were taking it back upstairs?" Art asked him.

"Changed my mind," Finn said with a wide grin. "I didn't know Ava was going to be here."

"She looks busy," Art tried again, but Finn turned back to me.

"You've got time to sit and chat with us for a minute, right?"

Truthfully, I did. I didn't have anything to write at the moment, as I was waiting for the gala this evening for my next article. Even still, I wanted to deny him, but the hopeful look on his face made me nod and close my laptop.

"Yeah, that's fine."

"See, I told you," Finn said smugly.

Art begrudgingly sat down next to his friend, and if I didn't want to see him as little as he wanted to see me, it would have been funny watching the satisfied gleam in Finn's eyes.

"So, tell me about yourself," Finn said as he settled back into the booth.

"What do you want to know?"

"If you could travel anywhere in the world, where would you want to go?"

"That's an odd first question," I said, finding myself relaxing with his easy attitude.

"You'd be surprised the stuff you can find out about someone from these types of questions," he said as he cut into his own omelet.

I stopped to think about it. "Switzerland," I said after a moment.

"Why?" he asked, popping a forkful of eggs into his mouth.

"There's a place there that looks like a town from a book that I love," I answered truthfully.

He smiled as he settled back again. "I like it."

"So, what did you learn about me?"

"You're a romantic, you're not afraid to be spontaneous, but you don't simply fly by the seat of your pants. You're also an avid reader."

"That's a lot to have learned from one question. Maybe you should start a palm reading business."

Finn laughed loudly and turned to Art. "I like her."

I felt heat flood my cheeks. I hadn't been looking for his approval, but it felt good to hear, until I noticed the way Art was glaring at him.

"What about you?" I asked, meaning to direct the question to Finn, but my gaze got caught on Art's. His eyes dropped to my mouth, and I subconsciously licked my lips. His gaze narrowed before slowly meeting my eyes again.

"I've already visited everywhere I want to be," Art said softly.

The air felt thick, and I swear my ears hollowed out as a clock on the wall began to *tick tick tick* louder. Had the furnace just turned on? It suddenly felt sweltering in here. Was I imagining it, or was Art leaning *closer, closer, closer—*

Finn laughed and I jerked back as the tension broke. "That's why no one likes you," he said as he elbowed Art. "You're rich and boring."

"Sorry, I gotta go," I said as I slid out of my seat, swinging my bag onto my shoulder.

"Nice to chat, see you tonight, Ava!" Finn called after me as I all but fled the room, leaving my breakfast untouched on the table.

22

Art

Why was every single thing about her so infuriating? When she had been talking to Finn about travel destinations, her voice had taken on that same quality as the first night we met, and all I wanted to do was get lost in her. She was beautiful, stunning, enigmatic. She was exactly what I was looking for, and I wanted to give in to the temptation to screw it all and take her anyway. Forget the hotel, forget the paper, just her and I.

But, unfortunately, something with the hotel was constantly needing my attention, and now I was sitting in a board meeting with a handful of our investors as Cain and I did our best to convince them not to pull their financial support.

Prior to the start of the meeting Cain had told me he would be there but mostly just for support, as it would be good for me to show that I was more than just the face of the company. Honestly, that took me by surprise, given his normal need to control things, but I was more than happy to prove to them that I was capable of this position.

Four people filed into the room, and I stood to shake each of their hands before they sat. I had attended enough functions with my mom to recognize their faces, but I didn't know any of them personally.

"Thanks for coming," I started. "I wanted to give you all an opportunity to share your concerns about these recent developments and to ask any questions."

The man to my right, Andrew, if I remembered correctly, nodded his appreciation. "I'm sure it doesn't come as much of a surprise that we are all a little nervous given the recent changes and circumstances surrounding the hotel."

"Lets cut to the chase, there have been two people murdered here in the last week, and sales have dramatically decreased since the news broke," the youngest of the group, Jeremy, said from my other side.

"Yes," I agreed. "And while that is definitely something to be concerned about, the New York police department have been working with us closely and have promised they are doing everything in their power to solve the case."

"Not to be insensitive," Carol mentioned from across from me, "But that doesn't really help us in the meantime with the lost sales."

"The Laurie has been doing extremely well, a week of bad press and decreased sales is not going to be enough to dismantle the empire that my mother built," I responded.

"And how do you know it's only going to be a week? Also, even when they catch whoever is doing this, that doesn't solve the concern of ownership passing over to you with you being so inexperienced," Andrew spoke again.

I glanced towards Cain. He sat with one eyebrow raised as if he too was waiting for the answer to this question. Asshole. I understood letting me take point, but he could at least step in with some support.

"Again, I understand the concern, but I do believe it is unfounded. The only position that has changed this week has been mine, the rest of my mother's staff and support are still here, and I have full confidence that things will continue to run smoothly as they have before. It takes more than one man to run a company, my mother did an excellent job, but she also surrounded herself with capable people, and I know that they will continue to be invaluable to me in this position."

I had hoped that would be enough to calm their fears, but they continued to go around in circles, asking question after question that I could not possibly have an answer to. When I finally left the meeting, I was just as discouraged as I had been before it even started.

We needed to find who was doing this, and soon.

23

Ava

I still couldn't believe Finn had convinced me to go to the gala with them tonight. I had actually started enjoying myself at breakfast, bantering back and forth with Finn, but the minute I remembered Art was there, it was like all of the oxygen had gotten sucked out of the room. He was this tall, angry cloud that threatened to pour on anyone in his path.

Okay, that was a bad analogy and immediately made me think of Art in a highly sexual position, which I was absolutely not going to even entertain.

I touched up my makeup one last time before heading downstairs. Vi had been right, this dress was stunning, and I was going to use every bit of it to my advantage.

I reached the lobby to find Arthur and Finn already standing by the doors talking. They were engrossed in their conversation, and I allowed myself the opportunity to check Art out. The way his black tux clung to his body was delicious. Every part of him was large, from his shoulders to his chest and thighs. He wasn't ripped like a model for a gym endorsement, but I honestly had never been one to go for the six pack anyway. I preferred his bulkiness, the feeling of being enveloped by someone, the heaviness when his body pressed into me from above.

He must have felt my gaze, because he swung his head toward me, and I tried to contain my racing pulse at the heat I saw as he not so subtly did his own examination of my body. Just as the atmosphere thickened to an almost unbearable level, Finn coughed, and I turned toward him.

"Gorgeous," he said, throwing me a dimpled smile. I dipped my head as I tried not to blush.

"Thank you, a friend of mine helped me pick it out," I gestured to the dress.

"Well, they have impeccable taste."

Finn and Vi. The thought sprung to my mind out of nowhere, and I stashed it away for later. That might be something I had to meddle in. I turned back toward Arthur and could have sworn anger simmered in his eyes as he stared at his friend. Finn didn't seem to notice but suddenly pulled out his phone.

"Man, I'm so sorry to ditch you last minute, but duty calls."

Arthur simply nodded as Finn turned to me, "It was great to see you again, Ava." He took my hand in his and pressed a kiss to my knuckles before seeming to skip away.

"I thought he was coming with us." I said in the silence that he left.

"It appears not. Shall we?" Arthur said, motioning to the door. Well, there went my plan to get information out of his friend. Then again, maybe if we were alone, Art would be more likely to talk to me.

I tried not to notice the hand he settled onto the small of my back as he guided me out of the hotel and to his waiting car. He opened the door for me like a perfect gentleman, and I slid into the back seat. He settled in beside me and his driver started off.

"So, your mom is the one who used to host this?" I said after a minute of awkward silence.

"Yes." This was going splendidly.

"You know, I'm really surprised."

When I didn't elaborate, he turned to look at me. "About what?"

"When I first met you in the bar, you seemed so fun, I never would have guessed you were just another boring ass."

He raised his eyebrows at me and then let out a loud laugh. "A boring ass? Is that what you think I am?"

"Anytime you're not trying to have sex, yeah."

His gaze slowly trailed down my body before his eyes met mine again. "I don't *try* to have sex, Ava."

I ignored him.

"Maybe it's the alcohol. That's the only thing that gives you a personality," I said with a decisive nod.

"Or maybe the alcohol is the only thing that makes me forget how much I can't stand you," he shot back.

"What? What did I ever do to you? Let me remind you, you were the one who approached me at the bar."

"Yes, before I knew you were only here to smear my name everywhere."

Guilt hit me, but I pressed on. "I'm here for a job. I'm sorry I can't quit my job over every hot guy I meet who wants his name kept out of the press."

"Oh, so you make a habit of sleeping with the men you write gossip about?" Something about the challenge in his voice enticed me.

"I don't see how that's any of your business."

"Maybe I want it to be my business." His confession appeared to shock him as much as it did me, and suddenly the air surrounding us felt too thick.

I took a deep breath, trying to slow my racing heart. Did I want that? For it to be his business? To acknowledge that I actually was interested in him and wanted to get to know him more than a random hookup?

There was something about him that drew me in, something that made me want to know more about who he was and what made him tick, more than just a job assignment. But he *was* a job assignment, and that complicated things too much.

Before I had a chance to reply, the car stopped in front of the hotel, saving me from having to come up with a response. Art exited and held out his hand for me. I placed my palm in his and let him pull me to my feet. I didn't let go until I got my balance and adjusted my dress, and when I attempted to pull away, he adjusted his grip and twined his fingers through mine before pulling me gently toward the door.

"My aunt died of leukemia when my mom was still quite young, and it hit her really hard," he said out of the blue.

Shocked by his words, I stayed silent as we stepped into the large, open space.

"After my mom established the Laurie and was looking for charities to support, she chose one that was near and dear to her and continued hosting these parties every year." Something about his tone made me want to pry, but I refrained.

"I'm sorry about your aunt," I said softly.

"Obviously, she wasn't the one who actually planned these events after the first couple times, it's all run by her team, so that's how this is still going on even after she's gone."

This was the second time he had completely brushed off a statement regarding a family passing. Not big on acknowledging emotions, got it.

"Did your mom pass from cancer as well?" I knew she had passed unexpectedly, but her team had done a great job keeping the cause of death quiet. Even Kim hadn't been able to find out how she died.

"No." A beat of silence. "She died from poisoning."

I stopped walking and gaped at him. "Poisoning?"

He tugged on my hand, and I resumed walking beside him as he led me to the center of the room where a platform and tables were set up.

"Botox. She apparently had a bad reaction to her most recent Botox injections. They're still not sure why." He delivered the news in such a matter of fact way, as if he wasn't talking about the death of the person who raised him. But maybe that's why. Maybe she hadn't raised him.

I knew their relationship didn't appear particularly close from anything I'd dug up so far, but maybe there were more problems than most people knew about.

"Wait here," he said as he left me near the stage and took the steps up. Only then did I notice that everyone appeared to be waiting for something and the hushed conversation quieted as he approached the microphone.

"Thank you, everyone, for coming. As you all know, this charity was very important to my mother, and I know she would be thrilled to see everyone continuing to support cancer research even in her absence."

Art spoke so confidently and eloquently, and I smiled at how comfortable he appeared. From everything he'd said so far, he had not been expecting to take over the company so soon, but he was going to do a great job here anyway.

He finished his brief speech and left the stage to a smattering of applause before the room began moving again as people walked by the raffle tables or enjoyed the free-flowing drinks. Art joined me again with two glasses of champagne, and I took mine from him with a murmured thanks.

Before I had time to comment on his speech, we were

approached by an older couple. Art kept one hand on the small of my back while he introduced me simply as "Ava" and made small talk with the couple in front of him.

The evening continued this way, Art always managing to include me in small ways as I sat back and watched him converse with those around us. As soon as one person left, another would arrive, making it clear that everyone here was attempting to get an in with the new CEO.

I felt a wave of sadness at the thought. What would it be like to have people only interested in what you could offer them instead of who you were? He had more money than most people would see in a lifetime, but along with that came being surrounded by sharks, circling and circling, just waiting for their chance to bite.

I was used to talking to people and generally thrived off of attention, but after only a couple of hours I was exhausted, and I hadn't even been the one talking all night.

During a brief break after the older woman in front of us moved on, Art turned to me.

"Ready to head out?"

"Absolutely."

"Thank God." Someone approached and he smiled at them before nodding towards the door. "I'm sorry, but I need to take my date home." When they tried to argue, he continued, "Feel free to make an appointment with my assistant, and I would love to sit down for a meeting." With that, he turned me toward the door and ushered me outside.

His car was waiting, and I realized he must have already told Alanzo that we were leaving. After we slid into the vehicle, Art leaned his head against the backrest with a sigh as he closed his eyes.

"I might envy your money, but I don't envy having to do that." I said, breaking the silence.

He cracked an eye open with a smile. "I don't envy me

either."

Before I had a chance to respond, he reached over and placed his palm on my bare thigh. I hadn't realized how much my slide into the car had revealed my leg, but looking down, my dress was doing its best job at creeping up on me. His thumb began slow circles on my leg, and my breath caught at the buzz it sent straight to my core. I looked up at him, but he had his eyes closed again as if he was unaware of what he was doing.

Ass. He knew exactly what he was doing.

I didn't break the silence, and he didn't stop his hand's slow exploration of my leg. Goosebumps broke over my skin, and I couldn't help but open my legs wider at his touch. His mouth lifted into a smirk, but his eyes remained closed, and after what felt like an eternity, we pulled into the hotel parking lot and the car stopped in front of the doors. Art finally opened his eyes and I asked, "Enjoy your nap?"

"Immensely."

He took my hand and led me toward the elevator. Once inside, he rubbed his thumb along the back of my hand in a gentle caress. "I have more of that champagne upstairs if you'd like."

I let myself debate for all of a second before I nodded, and he swiped his card for his suite. When the doors opened, he led me inside, and I took in the spacious level. It was an open concept with a kitchen to the left, living area directly ahead, and a hallway to the right that presumably led to bedrooms. I didn't have to wait for long to find out, as he took me into the hallway and pulled me along to the last door, which opened into a spacious room with a sitting area, massive bed, and bar.

"Welcome to my humble abode," he said with a flourish.

24

Art

While Ava looked around my space, I took a moment to walk to the bar and pour us both a glass of champagne. I didn't know what they had been serving tonight, but I knew that this stuff was good.

I reached her side, and she took the glass with a small smile. I hadn't been planning my confession earlier, but it was true. I couldn't get her out of my head. I didn't want to keep doing this back and forth of avoiding her all day long just to dream about her at night. I wasn't asking for a relationship here, but she lived in the same building for God's sake. We should at least take advantage of that.

While she hadn't said anything in response to my outburst, the way our conversation flowed and how she stuck to my side the rest of the night gave me hope that she might be on board. Plus, she was here now.

"This is my favorite part," I said as I walked toward my balcony. She followed me, and I moved the curtain and slid open the door, stepping out into the cool night air. Looking out, the city sparkled below us, with people still rushing about like they did at all hours. She came up beside me and breathed out as she looked down.

"Wow. I can see why."

We stood there for several moments, just looking out and drinking. Her faint perfume wafted toward me, and I set my empty glass on the railing in front of us. She looked up at me, and seeing those red lips open on a slight inhale, I couldn't help but close the distance. She took a step back as I caged her in until her back was against the wall.

"This dress really is stunning," I said as I traced one of the silver straps.

"Thank you, Finn seemed to like it too," she said with a smile.

"Please don't fucking talk about another guy right now. Or ever," I growled.

"Possessive much?"

"Are you trying to get yourself into trouble, love?"

"Depends, what does trouble look like?"

I took her glass from her hand and dropped it onto the ground, where it shattered. She let out a small scream, and I grabbed her hands and pinned them above her head with one of mine.

"I really don't think you're ready to find out."

She arched off the wall and nipped at my bottom lip, making me groan. "Fuck, Ava."

"What, you gonna break some more wine glasses?"

"No, I'm gonna fuck you until the only cock you ever dream about is mine."

I reached down and gripped her thighs, lifting her up and carrying her back into my room and to my bed. She wrapped her legs around me, and I set her down in front of the bed.

"Turn around."

I thought she was going to argue, but she complied

without a word, and I reached up and traced her shoulder blades before grasping the tab of her zipper. She sucked in a small breath at the light touch, and I took my time slowly lowering the zipper until her entire back was exposed. I reached up and slid the straps off her shoulders and the dress fell, pooling at her feet and leaving her in nothing but her thong.

Tracing her hips with my thumbs, goosebumps appeared on her skin.

"I fucking love these," I said, touching the dimples on her lower back. "Bend over."

She complied again, resting her hands on the bed, and I reached forward and pulled her thong over her perfect ass, dropping it on the floor with her dress. I sank to my knees behind her and ran my hands over her round cheeks before burying my face between her legs. She moaned and jerked from the intrusion of my tongue, but I held her in place and absolutely consumed her.

"You taste like heaven," I said, pulling away for a second. "I could drown in the taste of you." Before she had a chance to respond, I was back at her clit. I could feel her body begin to tremble uncontrollably, and I plunged a finger inside. She moaned and writhed, and I added another finger, pumping in and out of her slowly.

"Art," she panted, and I moaned against her at the sound of my name on her lips.

"Please, oh fuck, please," she begged.

I nipped at her swollen clit, and she came apart, clenching around my fingers, where I continued to stroke her until she squirmed off me. She went to turn around, but I stopped her with a hand in her hair.

"I'm not done."

"I don't know if my legs can hold me much longer."

"They can and they will."

I stood and reached around her to grab something from my nightstand before moving to stand behind her again. Stepping out of my pants, I slid the cock ring and condom on before grabbing her, using her hips to grind her against me as we moaned in unison at the friction. I slid my dick against her entrance. "You're soaked for me, baby."

She only moaned in response, and I slowly slid inside her, inch by slow inch as she writhed against me, attempting to sink me deeper, but I held her firm.

"So greedy, little bird." I reached down and pressed the button on my cock ring, and it began vibrating as I pushed all the way inside her. She gasped and bucked off me, and I let her get all the way to my tip before slamming back into her to the hilt.

"Art!" she squealed, and I pulled out before slamming back in.

"Look how good you take me, baby girl. You're so fucking good at taking my cock."

She moaned at the praise, and it only took a few more thrusts before she came apart again, clenching around me and screaming my name.

I held her against me, and the tight heat and vibration sent me tumbling over the edge after her. As she crumpled to the bed, I kept my grip on her with one hand and myself from crushing her with the other.

We sat there panting while I caught my breath before I picked her up and deposited her on the bed unceremoniously. Her hair was wild from where I had fisted it, and her cheeks had the prettiest flush to them. I crawled up next to her and couldn't help but plant a soft kiss to her mouth. She smiled sleepily at me with a look of pure contentment that did weird things to my heart.

"What time is it?" she murmured.

I reached for my phone.

"One a.m."

"I should go," she groaned as she started to sit up.

"Stay," I said, grabbing her hand to stop her. "If you want," I added at her look of hesitation. She seemed to contemplate before finally collapsing back onto my pillows.

"Only 'cause your bed is so stinking soft."

"Whatever helps you sleep at night," I smirked.

She settled in, and I pulled the blankets up over her before draping my arm across her.

"I hope you're not opposed to cuddling, cause you're not gonna keep me away from these curves," I said, running my hand over her ass.

"Only for tonight," she said with a yawn.

It was cute how she was playing hard to get. As if I was going to let her go now that I had her. She'd get used to the idea, and for now I'd let her pretend that she wasn't utterly and completely mine.

25

Ava

I awoke to the feeling of a heavy presence on my hip and I opened my eyes to see sunlight pouring into an unfamiliar room. My brain took a second to catch up before I remembered last night and Art asking me to stay the night. Fuck. I never stayed the night.

Who cared if I was technically only staying downstairs from him right now, I hadn't slept next to someone since my last relationship, and this made everything feel—more.

I slowly rolled onto my back and glanced over to find him still asleep, breathing deeply with his arm draped over me. I oh so carefully slid out from under his grip and looked around the room. Our dress clothes from last night still lay on the floor. Not a great option.

I swiveled around the rest of the room, thankful for the morning sunlight peering through the shades illuminating enough of the space for me to see a walk-in closet on my side of the bed. I moved that way and tried not to salivate at the storage I saw. What I wouldn't give for a beautiful walk-in closet like this.

My gaze passed over his pressed suits, shelves full of watches, rows of shoes, and finally landed on hangers with what looked like normal t-shirts. I pulled off the one nearest me and slipped it on before finding a pair of sweatpants. I tried not to imagine how delicious he would look in a t-shirt and sweats, with tousled morning hair and sleep still in his voice. Nope, not going there. I'd already stayed longer than I should have.

I snuck back through the room and quietly grabbed my clothes off the floor before sneaking out. As I exited the hallway, I immediately cursed open concepts when I saw the older woman at the kitchen stove.

"Good morning, miss, I'm just getting started on breakfast if you'd like something."

"No, thank you," I mumbled before fleeing into the elevator. Great, just your casual walk of shame.

I made it back to my room without running into anyone else and ordered room service before pulling out my computer and checking my emails.

Kim. *Anything new to add in regard to Arthur? I'm counting on you. If you're not up for the job, I can send Candice over.*

Shit. *Nope, I've got something on Laurie's cause of death*, I typed up and sent before I had a chance to second guess myself.

A reply came in less than a minute later. When did this lady sleep? *Perfect, I'll expect to have it by the end of the day.*

What was I doing? Art was going to hate me.

I scrubbed my face. I'd never run into a situation like this before. I'd never gotten attached to someone that prevented me from doing my job. That was all this was. A job. And yet the guilt I felt threatened to choke me when I imagined Art seeing the article and feeling instantly betrayed.

This was his mom. He had trusted me with this

information. Had given it to me after telling me he wanted something more than just sex. I'd pushed him to prove it by talking to me, and he had, and now was I really going to use that against him?

But what choice did I have? I had to give Kim the story. Maybe I could give her this and that would be enough. Breaking the news on Laurie's cause of death was huge. No one else had caught wind of it, it would be big. It had to be enough.

And if it's not? It would be. *And if Art doesn't forgive you?* He would. And even if he didn't, I didn't need his forgiveness. I didn't owe him anything. He knew exactly why I was here and what I was here to do.

And yet, despite telling myself that, I couldn't get rid of the guilt nagging me and leaving a bitter taste in my mouth.

<h1 style="text-align:center">26</h1>

Art

I awoke to the smell of bacon and an empty bed. Sometime last night or this morning, Ava had left, and I cursed my ability to sleep through a hurricane for not noticing. Thankfully, I knew exactly where she currently lived.

I dressed in something casual and exited to the kitchen bar, where Angie had a breakfast feast set out.

"Good morning," she murmured before taking a plate and excusing herself from the room.

I didn't mind, as I filled a plate and brought it to my computer.

So far, news of the second murder hadn't been made public yet, but I knew it was only a matter of time. While the transition of the company from my mom to me couldn't be blamed for these deaths, having a serial killer rampant in your hotel didn't do great things for the company's image. We would definitely be needing some damage control.

I pulled up my emails and began responding to the important ones and accepting meetings to add to my calendar. I still had yet to hear anything new from the detectives, and while I liked to go with the rule of no news is good news, in this instance, I couldn't help but think about what this meant for the investigation.

The same thoughts that had plagued me for the last week resurfaced. How had someone managed to come into the hotel and murder not one but two guests? We had an amazing security system, how had they managed to get around undetected?

Did the killer have someone on the inside? Did I have a disgruntled employee willing to sell information? Or someone with intimate knowledge doing it themselves?

An alert came through on my computer, and I switched to the news outlet.

Former CEO of Laurie hotel's cause of death exposed

Laurie Michaels, an entrepreneur and the CEO of the popular hotel chain, passed unexpectedly last week. Her company has since passed to her son amidst questions and rumors regarding her death. Someone close to the deceased exposed recently that her death was entirely preventable. The former hotel owner died from a complication related to her frequent Botox injections. While Botox poisoning is rare, there are several recorded cases of death from unlicensed injections and compounds. Was Micheals getting injections in a less than reputable center? Is the Michaels empire not as secure as it seems?

My stomach knotted and my blood ran cold with every word that I read. I finally reached the bottom and read the signature. *Ava Schmidt.*

I was going to be sick.

Here I had spent the night with her, took her to the gala, talked about my family, thought that maybe we were starting something. Maybe we were more than just sex. But that's all it had been for her. She'd used me. Like every other person who had come before her, every girl who just wanted a chance to sleep with me in hopes of getting something from me.

Not that I hadn't been a willing participant in our exchanges, but fuck, I thought she was with me because she enjoyed it not just because she wanted a story out of.

They were all the same, and I was an idiot for ever thinking otherwise.

27

Ava

Kim was thrilled when she read my piece. I finished it and sent it off before I could second guess myself, and I got a shining stamp of approval from her. My job was safe for another day.

After getting my work done, I texted Vi to see how her meeting with Winnie went. She said she'd prefer to talk about details over drinks tonight, which I was more than happy to agree to. We decided on a time and place, and I took a nice long shower. When I got out, I was visually putting my outfit together when I realized that I had forgotten my heels in Art's room.

I mentally berated myself, such a rookie mistake, and considered texting him, but we hadn't texted since that first time, and using his number now felt even more embarrassing than showing my face for some reason.

After going through every possibility I could think of for getting them back, I decided short of going out and buying another pair, I had to make my way to his suite. Maybe I'd get lucky and he wouldn't be there and his housekeeper would answer instead.

I really shouldn't be this nervous to see him, this was the third time we'd hooked up. But something about last night felt bigger. More intimate. And now with this article hanging between us… I shook my head at my cowardice. I had made a choice, and I would now face the consequences. Regardless of the butterflies he gave me, he was just a guy.

I made my way to the elevator and pressed the button for his floor. A polite voice asked me my name, and after giving it, the elevator began moving. It felt weird to be coming back here so soon and without Art. The doorman hadn't specified if Art was here, so I had no idea what to expect.

When the doors opened and I stepped onto his floor, I was a little surprised to see him sitting on his couch with his laptop and a stack of papers. He didn't acknowledge me when I walked in, even though I was sure he'd heard the elevator arrive. I stood several feet away in awkward silence for a few moments before clearing my throat.

"Sorry, I forgot to grab my shoes this morning."

He motioned to the table without looking up, and I followed the gesture to see them sitting on the wooden surface. I awkwardly walked over to retrieve them, feeling a weird sort of tension suffocating the air between us. I didn't know what I'd been expecting, but it definitely wasn't this. Maybe I'd thought he would ask me why I snuck out and ask me to stay. Maybe he'd yell at me for using him for information on his mom. But not this icy silence. I picked up my shoes and made my way back toward the elevator. He remained still, making no sound except the *tap, tap,* of his computer.

"Okay then. Sorry to bother you."

His jaw clenched, but he again refused to look up. Now I was starting to feel pissed. Last night he was fucking me and begging me to stay and now he couldn't even stand to look at me? It made me feel used and gross.

"Is everything okay?"

Finally, he looked up at me, and I expected anger or hostility, but instead I saw cold indifference.

"Why wouldn't it be?"

"It's just that you're acting completely different from last night."

"And?"

I didn't know what to say. And what, Ava? You expected some sort of commitment just because he held you as you fell asleep? Maybe. *You're the one who snuck out this morning*, I reminded myself. But this wasn't about logic. This was my emotions, and the fact that he had seemed to get what he wanted from my body and was now over it stung and brought back way too many bad memories.

When I didn't respond, his lip turned up in a sneer that transformed his face in a way I had never seen before.

"Oh, you expected sweet nothings? You wanted me to hold your hand and tell you how much I liked your pussy?" he scoffed.

My stomach knotted at his vulgar words. Ouch.

"Sorry, sweetheart, the sex was good, but I have nothing else to offer you, and there's *definitely* nothing else I want from you."

His words pierced exactly as I was sure he intended them to.

"Is this about the piece I wrote about your mom? I'm sorry if it hurt you, you know I'm here to write about the company, I never hid that from you."

A flash of anger sparked in his gaze but then died just as quickly as it had come.

"I don't care what you write about me or my mom. For me to be hurt, I'd actually have to care, which I don't. You were an itch I wanted to scratch, and I did."

He shrugged as if he didn't have a care in the world. "You're hot, but don't mistake this for anything more than physical attraction."

The words burned all the way down to my gut, and I nodded without a word and hurried for the elevator. Somehow, I made it all the way back to my room before the tears fell. I didn't even know exactly why I was crying. Embarrassment, hurt, anger? I hadn't expected a goddamn proposal, but I'd thought that I meant something to him. Not that I was just an "itch to scratch."

I let myself wallow in pity for another few moments before pulling myself together and texting Vi that I was going to be heading over sooner than planned. I needed to drown my sorrows and forget about Arthur Michaels.

28

Art

As soon as Ava left my apartment, I deflated. The last thing I'd been expecting as I did my morning scheduling was for her to show up. I'd already been stewing about what I'd say to her, and when she marched in as if nothing was wrong and she hadn't just splashed my name all over the news, I couldn't help but lash out.

Was it right? No. Did it make me feel better? Temporarily.

And now I had to attempt to move on from that as I prepared to meet with detective Sheridan again. He had called me almost as soon as she left to let me know they had a description of a possible suspect that they wanted my opinion on. Maybe we were finally getting somewhere.

The detectives arrived, and Angie showed them into my office space, which they were becoming all too familiar with.

"Mr. Michaels, thank you for your time."

I nodded but didn't say anything. I was already wary after the interrogation at the police station, and I had Lacy on standby if I felt like I needed her at any point.

"Great news, your alibis checked out for both murders," he started.

"Good," I responded curtly.

"More good news, as I told you on the phone, we were able to get a description of someone who may have been responsible for wiping the security footage."

He had told me that over the phone, but I was still cautious about what that meant.

"Can I ask where you got the description from?"

"Certainly. Your head of security gave us the list of people who were working during the times of the murders. When we talked to one of them, a guy by the name of Sean, he mentioned someone coming in the night of the second murder with an order from you to check the security footage. It appears that he logged in and wiped the recording from that night." Relief washed over me. Finally, we had something to go on.

"Are you able to track him by his login?"

"We attempted to, but he used your credentials."

Red hot fury shot through me. He had somehow gotten my credentials? How? Who was this?

"As I said, your alibi is solid, so we believe someone took your information and used it to delete the evidence."

"You said you had a description?" I asked, trying to contain the heat rolling through me.

"Yes," he said as he laid out a sketch on the table of a bald man with brown eyes and a goatee. I had been hopeful that I would know him or at least recognize him from someone on staff here, but nothing about him seemed familiar.

"I have no idea who that is."

Sheridan nodded as he leaned back in his chair but left the sketch on my desk. "We were afraid of that. After we showed his picture to your head of security, he also denied recognizing him. We will continue searching, but in the meantime, we suggest changing all of your login information."

"Done."

"Another thing," he said, and the tone of his voice caused me to tense. Whatever was coming next was not going to be good.

"We are going to have to release a police statement soon. I know this will most likely cause issues for you in regard to the hotel business, so I wanted to give you that heads up."

"Thank you for the warning," I said, as the men stood to exit.

"You can keep the sketch, and if anyone comes to mind or you hear anything else, please let us know."

I agreed, not that I had much of a choice, and the men left. I sent a message to Lacy to let her know what the detectives had wanted, and I also sent a message to the board of directors, informing them of the police statement.

After moving things around on my calendar, I began preparing for another business meeting this evening. A son of one of our investors who had not been able to meet yesterday had reached out with a request for drinks. With any luck, I would be able to finish today better than it had started.

29

Ava

Vi wanted to meet at a nicer club today, and I wasn't about to complain as long as they had alcohol. I arrived before she did and found us a booth to settle into while I waited. It was early enough that the crowd was light, and this wasn't the type of place people came to dance and grind against each other, so the people watching was subpar. Regardless, I enjoyed my drink, watching the people around me and scrolling on my phone until Vi arrived. By the time she got there, I was a little tipsy and feeling much less ready to cry all over her. Instead, I forced her to tell me all about her meeting with Winnie.

"It was amazing! She was so wonderful and kind and offered me a chance to dance for her on another date!"

I squealed and pulled her into a hug, which earned us a couple glances from those around us but I didn't care. She was doing it.

"I knew she'd love you! You're going to have a lead role in no time."

She laughed as she hugged me back. "I wouldn't get too

excited. I still have to audition. She might hate me."

"Impossible, no one hates you."

Another laugh. "I'm sorry, but I don't take ballet advice from you."

I wrinkled my nose at her but nodded anyway.

"Fair, I might not have an athletic bone in my body, but still, I'm confident that she'll love you and offer you a position the minute she sees you perform."

Vi gave me a small smile and I could see the excitement there mixed with the nerves.

"Now stop stalling and tell me what happened," she prodded.

I swirled the ice in the bottom of my glass to avoid looking at her. "Nothing really happened. I forgot my shoes at Art's this morning." I ignored her exclamation. "So, I went to get them from him and he basically made it clear that he wasn't interested in hooking up with me again."

"And?"

"And nothing, we haven't known each other long, there was no commitment, I was just disappointed."

"I know you better than that. He said something else, or you wouldn't have cared that much."

"He might have said something about how he liked my body but that's where his interest ended or something."

I finally looked up at her and saw anger reflected in her eyes.

"What an ass. Seriously, what gives him the right to treat you like that? Just cause he has money? Ignorant pig," she muttered with a scowl.

I sighed. "I did write an article about his mother and her cause of death that had been kept private. He does have a right to be pissed."

Vi nodded slowly. "Okay, maybe he has a right to be angry, but that does not give him the right to insult you like that."

"Yeah, well, it's over now. I can't imagine Kim has that much more for me now that I've covered what we can of his story."

"Don't say that," Vi grumbled. "It's been so nice to have you in the city. And like I've been telling you for years, I would love to share an apartment with you."

"Especially if you get this ballet gig. You'll be able to afford our own penthouse," I teased, trying to lighten the mood again.

We shared another laugh, and I swayed a little as I stood, "I need to use the restroom."

"Right behind you," Vi said as she stood on much steadier legs. We had just finished and were about to head back to our table when a tall man with sandy colored hair and stunning blue eyes almost ran me over. He grasped my biceps to steady me, and I took in his crisp button down and slacks before meeting his gaze. He was a foot taller than me, and I had to tilt my head to meet his gaze.

"My apologies," he said as he released my arms. His voice was deep with a slight accent that I couldn't place, and it washed over me like velvet. I was a sucker for accents.

"It's my fault," I said, "I wasn't paying attention to where I was going."

"Still, I should have been more aware. Let me buy you a drink, it's the least I can do."

I glanced over at Vi, and she nodded at me with a smile, so I agreed and followed him to the corner of the bar. I was already feeling a little unsteady, so I probably didn't need another drink, but hey, it was free.

After placing our order, which I hadn't bothered to listen to, he rested his forearm on the bar and leaned against it casually. "I'm Mark, by the way."

"Ava," I said, shaking his offered hand.

"Ava," he said slowly, as if he was tasting the word.

"Reminds me of a goddess."

I giggled, although I was sure it was a line he used fairly often.

"Sorry, Mark doesn't scream 'god' to me."

He smirked, "No? Pity."

The bartender handed us our drinks, and Mark wrapped a hand around my wrist and tugged me gently towards the dimly lit corner. It was quieter over here, and he kept tugging until he was leaning against the wall. I took a sip of my drink and we fell into an uncomfortable silence. I cleared my throat, but before I had a chance to thank him for the drink and leave, he was pulling me into his broad chest.

His hand wrapped around the back of my neck, and he pulled my face toward him as he dipped and crushed his lips to mine. I placed my free hand on his chest and attempted to push away, and when he pulled back, I thought he understood until he spun us around so that my back was pressed against the wall, and he was pressing his body into me.

My hands, including my glass, were trapped between us as his hands roamed roughly up and down my body. I squirmed in an attempt to push him off me but only succeeded in feeling his erection press into me. My movements became frantic as he pinched and squeezed my ass and bruised my lips between his. He finally pulled back enough for me to squeak out, "What are you doing?"

"Giving you what you wanted," he said crudely.

"Excuse me?"

"Oh, don't play shy with me," his voice turned condescending. "You were giving me those doe eyes and accepted my drink."

"Are you fucking kidding me? I accepted your drink, I didn't give you permission to grope me!"

"As if I need your permission," he snarled before stepping

into me again to grip my ass and neck. I began to scratch and claw, but his grip was like iron, and his hand moved from my ass toward my vagina as terror ran through me. How was no one seeing this?

I attempted to scream against his lips, but he swallowed the sound. He was so much bigger than me, even if I had been sober, I wouldn't have been able to fight him off. His callous fingers groped my vagina, when suddenly a voice broke through my panic as someone bellowed, "Get off her!"

30

Art

What was supposed to be a stress-free dinner and drinks to convince yet another investor not to pull their funds had quickly derailed. My associate had left me for the restroom, and it had been long enough that I was convinced he had ditched and left me with the bill.

Mark was a slimy piece of shit, and I didn't know why my mom had ever started a relationship with his company, but, nonetheless, I had no reason to burn bridges, so here I was, playing nice. At least he could have the decency not to leave without telling me.

Our server must have been tied up with some other expensive table, as I hadn't seen him in a hot minute, so I opted to leave our table and go to the bar myself for another drink while I waited. The place was starting to get crowded as more and more business meetings took place or people just came to unwind, and while waiting, my gaze landed on two figures in the shadows, and I was pretty sure one of them was Mark. He left me to go hookup with someone, really?

Figured. I made my way closer to his area of the bar and ordered. Maybe I'd wander a little too close and make things nice and uncomfortable for him. Or maybe I'd just leave and he could find out that I was gone when he was done with whatever this was.

By the time my drink was empty, I had decided I'd leave him here, until I heard what sounded like a pained cry from the shadows. A shiver passed over me. No one should be making that noise when being kissed. I walked closer, not caring if he got pissed at the intrusion or if it was just a weird misunderstanding, and then I noticed the blonde hair that haunted my dreams. I was suddenly seeing red and wishing that I had my pistol on me.

"Get off her!"

Mark turned at my harsh tone and chuckled when he saw me. "Arthur—"

He didn't have time for another word as my fist connected with his mouth. My hand stung and blood sprayed from his mouth as he cried out and doubled over. But I wasn't done. One brief look at Ava's white face and fear stricken eyes and nothing would have been able to stop me from going after Mark right then.

My other fist connected with his stomach and then his nose, where I felt a crunch. He screamed in earnest, and only when I felt a shaky hand on my arm did I still.

"Art, we need to go."

I glanced back to Ava before noticing the stares and the crowd that was starting to form. I couldn't force myself to care. When I made no effort to move, she grabbed my hand and pulled me away from Mark and toward the door. I let her drag me through the crowd, and once we were outside, she asked softly, "Is Alanzo here?"

I shook my head and attempted to focus on her instead of how badly I wanted to go finish what I had started. "No, I drove tonight." I looked over at her and noticed how badly she was shaking. "Are you alone?"

"No, I came with Vi." She paused. "But I don't want her to see me like this," she said in a whisper. "I'll just text her."

I nodded. "Do you want a ride?"

"Please," she whispered again, and I wanted to wrap my arms around her at the broken sound. Instead, I gently interlaced our fingers and steered her toward my car.

I let her into the passenger's side and slid behind the wheel, keeping one hand in hers. We didn't talk as I drove us back and parked in the underground garage. I led her up to her room and waited while she swiped her keycard. Once we were finally inside, I steered her toward the couch and sat down next to her. She looked down at my hand that had barely left hers this whole time. "You're bleeding."

"It's fine."

"Did you break anything?"

I knew she was referring to me. I had hopefully broken the fucker's nose, but thanks to my regular boxing with Finn, I knew how to punch without breaking any of my own bones.

"I'll be fine," I said again.

She continued to stare at my hand. "He could call the cops on you."

"He won't."

Finally, she looked up and met my gaze. "Why not? Do you know him?" she said, and the betrayal in her voice made me want to burn the hotel to the ground.

Instead, I tried to push aside thoughts of my own need for vengeance and focused on her. "Yes," I answered honestly. "He's the son of one of my mom's investors. He's a piece of shit, and someone should have broken his face a long time ago."

I hoped for a smile or laugh or some sort of acknowledgment, but instead she stared off at a spot on her wall with a vacant look in her eyes.

"Are you okay?" I asked. Dumb question, but I didn't know what else to say.

"I don't know what happened," she said in another broken whisper. "One second he was buying me a drink, and then—" Her voice trailed off and I again had to resist the urge to pull her into my arms.

"Do you want me to call Vi for you?"

She quickly shook her head.

"Are you sure?" I pressed. I didn't know her best friend well, but I was sure she would be a better person to be here during this time than I would.

"She'd just feel guilty."

When I looked at her in confusion, she went on. "We ran into him together, and she encouraged me to go over with him. Not that it's her fault," she rushed out. "But she would feel like it was and— I Just don't want to have to tell her about it right now."

I nodded and gently rubbed my finger over her knuckles. She glanced down at our hands.

"Thanks for driving me back." She stood and wrapped her arms around herself in a clear dismissal.

"Of course. Are you sure there isn't someone I can call to come hang out with you tonight? I don't think you should necessarily be alone here."

"Why do you care?" she asked, without meeting my eyes.

"What do you mean?" I said as I felt my anger rekindle at her words.

"Why would you care if I'm here alone? I appreciate the ride, and you were being all Mr. gentlemanly, but nothing physical is happening here."

"You think I want to fuck you?" I hissed in disbelief.

"No, but you're the one who made it clear this is just physical."

Ouch. But she was right. I had made her feel like the only thing I wanted out of this was her body. What a dick.

"You're right, I did say that." She nodded to herself as if to confirm her suspicions. "But I was lying. To you, to myself. I was pissed about the article you wrote, and I lashed out."

"Well, it doesn't matter. You can leave now."

"Ava…"

"Why, Art, why does it matter?" Her voice came out broken and pleading, and I couldn't stop the words from tumbling out as I surged to my feet.

"Because I fucking care. Because I can't get you out of my head. Because even when I'm pissed about you writing stuff about me I want to be with you, not just sex but I want to talk to you and make you laugh and get to learn more about you and see your smile light up the room."

I took a step toward her but stopped myself from reaching for her. She deserved her space, I wasn't going to pressure her into something, especially not right now. But I had to get through to her.

"And you were right. I knew you were here to write about me and the company, it was my choice to share what I did with you, and you gave me no promises of what you would or wouldn't do with it. I was a dick."

"I'm sorry for writing that about your mom." A tear slipped free and rolled down Ava's cheek, and my heart broke at the sight. "Kim has been pressuring me to write something, find something, and it wasn't personal, but I shouldn't have taken advantage of your trust like that."

I opened my mouth to respond, but she held up her hand and I stopped.

"I don't believe it, that you can't run the company. I think you're amazing, I think you're going to make a great CEO," she said with a fresh wave of tears.

"Honey, please don't cry over me." Another sob broke free

and I couldn't help it when I finally opened up my arms. "Come here."

I watched the struggle in her eyes before she stepped into my embrace and wrapped her arms around me as she let herself fall apart.

"Shhh, honey. I'm sorry, I'm so sorry," I said as I stroked her back.

"I was scared. I was so fucking scared." She said between sobs. "I didn't think anyone was gonna hear me."

"I'm so sorry I wasn't there sooner. I promise you he'll never hurt you again."

She continued to sob, and I held her as her shaking subsided. After a minute, she finally stepped back and wiped her tear streaked face.

"What can I get for you?" I asked, desperate to help in any way that I could.

"Stay with me. Please?"

"Of course."

I followed her into the bedroom, and she stopped in the doorway, turning to me, "I need to shower."

"I'll be right here when you're done."

She nodded gratefully, and as soon as I heard the shower turn on, I pulled up an old contact.

"Toni," the female voice on the other end of the line answered.

"Hey, it's Arthur Michaels."

"Art, it's been awhile." Indeed, I hadn't talked to her since boarding school.

"Are you still in the technology business?" I asked.

A moment of silence.

"Not sure what you mean."

"I need some help. I have someone that I need some dirt dug up on. Anything illegal or unethical that could be shared to the public. I can pay handsomely."

There was another moment of silence and I wondered if she had disconnected when she finally answered. "I can handle it. Send me the information."

"Thank you," I said before she hung up and I sent off Mark's contact information. I had meant what I said. He would never be in a position to hurt her again. He'd been the catalyst to his own demise when he decided to touch what wasn't his.

By the time Ava came out of the bathroom in an oversized t-shirt, I was already in my boxers and undershirt. She slipped under the sheets with me, and I held her to my chest as she drifted off to sleep.

31

Ava

I woke up to the sound of soft snores and the feeling of Art's arm draped over me. He was a huge snuggler, which was a cute trait. I still had the remnants from yesterday's headache, and my eyes felt swollen, but I was lighter now than I had been when I went to sleep. It had felt good to get those unspoken words out in the open.

I enjoyed hanging out with him when he wasn't being hot and cold. And if I was honest, it had been fear that had pushed me to write that article. Fear that without it, Kim would fire me, yes, but also fear of getting too close to him. Going to sleep in his bed and waking up next to him had scared me, and maybe part of me writing the article was self-sabotage to make sure I ended whatever we were before it could go any further.

I rolled over as gently as I could and watched Art as he continued to sleep. A piece of his dark hair fell over his face, and I reached up to brush it out of his eyes. He grumbled and attempted to pull me closer. I giggled and pushed back against his chest. He cracked his eyes open.

"Rude," he said as he tugged me closer again, and I lost the fight and slid into his chest. He nuzzled his face into my neck and pressed a kiss to my skin. Sleepy Art might be my favorite. His mouth continued its trail down my neck but halted when I swatted him. "Stop."

He did, albeit reluctantly. "Why?" he grumbled again.

I forced some space between us so I could look into his face. "I don't do this." When his eyebrow cocked, I continued. "I don't do sleepovers."

He propped himself up on an elbow. "You want me to leave?"

"No." He gave a satisfied smirk at my quick response.

"I enjoy having you here," I continued, and he reached forward to trace a finger down my bare arm, causing a shiver. "But what is this?" I finished.

His hand stilled. "What do you mean?"

"We were having angry sex, then you beat someone up for me," his jaw ticked at the reminder of last night, "and then you stayed over last night, I just don't know what we're doing here."

"We're hanging out."

"Exclusively?" I pressed. His eyes darkened.

"Were you planning on going out with someone else?"

I had no intention of going out with anyone else right now, but the angry look on his face at the idea did bring me some sort of satisfaction. "I mean if the occasion arises..."

He gave me all of a second before rolling on top of me and pressing me into the bed beneath him.

"Did you get a good look at Mark's face?" he asked, his voice low.

I nodded as the image of his nose pouring blood popped back into my mind.

"That is what will happen to anyone else who touches

you."

"Overprotective much?"

His face didn't show a speck of humor. "Don't push me."

"You can't just go beating up anyone who touches me. That's illegal."

"Watch me."

Honestly, after last night, I believed him. And with his millions, I didn't doubt he could get away with it, too. Corrupt legal system and all that.

He began to grind against me but stopped again when I put my hand on his chest. "If we're going to give this a go, we can't just have sex."

"The fuck we can't."

I laughed and swatted him. "We already know we have great physical chemistry. That's never been our problem. Communication, on the other hand..."

He stared down at me with a raised brow.

"I want to get to know you, go on dates, not just spend time in bed," I continued.

"It doesn't have to just be bed. It could be a car. Couch. Elevator. Shower." He punctuated each word with a soft kiss, and I groaned as I tried to stop myself from writhing beneath him.

"I mean it!"

He finally pulled back and flopped onto the bed next to me. "Fine. I have work to do this morning, but tonight. You. Me. Dinner. I'll pick you up at five."

I leaned up to kiss him and then shimmied out of the bed before he could grab me. "I'll be waiting," I said with a smile as I closed the bathroom door behind me. I turned on the shower and laughed as I heard a loud groan from the other room. This was going to be fun.

After a nice long shower, I exited to find my room empty and grabbed my phone to call Vi. She answered after the first ring.

"What happened?"

I settled onto my bed in my towel and prepared myself to rehash last night.

"Your text wasn't very helpful," she continued. "Last I saw you were heading to the bar with that cute guy, and then all of a sudden people were yelling and you left and I was freaking out."

Guilt filled my stomach. "I'm sorry. His name was Mark. After he bought me a drink he got handsy, he wouldn't take no for an answer, and Art saw us, and I'm pretty sure he broke his nose."

"WHAT?" I had to pull my phone away to save my eardrums. "I'm coming over right now. Are you okay? Why was Arthur there? How did you get home? Why didn't you tell me? I would have come over last night. That piece of shit, I'm going to find out where he lives."

"I'm okay. Art stopped him before he could do anything." Silence. "Really, I'm okay. Just freaked out and shaken up."

"I'm so sorry, I never should have left you with him."

"Stop it, I'm a big girl, it was my decision. Last time I take a free drink from someone for a while though," I said, trying to bring back some humor to the conversation.

"Do you want me to come over there? We can order takeout and look up his information to burn his house down."

I laughed and stretched out on the bed. "As great as that sounds, I have some work to do, and then Art is taking me on a date tonight."

There was a beat of silence, and I chewed on my lip as I waited for a response.

"What do you mean he's taking you on a date?"

"You know, restaurant, dinner, wine," I said with a laugh. She didn't join in.

"Why?"

"Why what?"

"Why would you go out with that ass?"

"Vi, he saved me from Mark. I'm not kidding, I'm pretty sure he punched him so hard he broke his nose."

"And that makes up for what he said to you?"

"Of course not," I sighed. How to explain this. "He brought me back home last night. We talked, I cried, he apologized, he stayed the night."

"So just like that, you've forgiven him."

"No. Well, maybe. I'm giving him a chance to make it up to me," I responded. "Plus, I have some making up to do to him too. I was a dick for writing that article about him."

"Hmm," she said, unconvinced.

"Can you please just be happy for me?"

"He's going to have to do a lot more than that for me to forgive him," she finally said.

I laughed again. "I'll be sure to let him know. Now, can you please help me decide what to wear?"

Vi continued to grumble into the phone, and I smiled at the sound. I appreciated her protectiveness and the fact that she always had my back. Everyone needed a Vi in their life. Now, onto the more pressing matter of my wardrobe.

32

Art

I spent the morning watching Mark's life crumble around him. This morning Mark had woken up to several of his private messages getting leaked, including conversations where he blatantly admitted to forcing himself on multiple women. The story had already begun to circulate and several of his victims had already come forward to press charges.

Not only that, but Mark's company had mysteriously hit financial troubles and was no longer able to be one of our highest investors. I felt a little bad for his mom, but anyone who raised a piece of shit human like Mark was also partially responsible for his actions.

By the time I began preparing for my date with Ava, I was feeling lighter than I had in a long while. I dressed in a nice pair of slacks and a button down and headed to her room. I had sent her a dress to wear for tonight, and I couldn't wait to see it on her. I knocked on her door, and a moment later she opened it, and I stepped back to take her in. The dress was gold with a plunging neckline and the smallest glitter when

136

the material shifted.

"Damn."

She smiled and swished her hips, and I whistled in appreciation.

"I just heard that our reservation was cancelled and we have to stay in tonight," I said with a shrug.

She laughed and swatted my arm with her matching clutch. "Since you spent what I can only imagine is a fortune on my dinner outfit, I really want to show it off."

"Fine," I grumbled as I offered my arm, and we started for the elevator. I took her out the front door and ushered her into my waiting car, then slid in after her and Alanzo took off. I settled my hand on her thigh and smiled in appreciation at her small intake of breath. I was thinking about seeing how far I could explore, when she broke the silence.

"Did you always want to take over the company?"

I stilled as I tried to think of how to answer. I knew she had done extensive research on me and already knew what college I attended, who I hung out with, what counties I lived in. Not everything could be found on paper, however.

"I don't know if I ever really thought about it. It was just always the expectation that I would take it over. My mom worked hard to build her empire, and she wasn't going to leave it to just anybody when she was done. That being said, she wasn't supposed to hand it off for at least another twenty years."

"I'm really sorry for her passing."

I shrugged. "It sounds terrible, but I never had a close relationship with her. She spent my entire childhood making something of herself, and while I appreciate the money and effort she put into it, I don't think I can ever remember a time that we hung out outside of charity events."

She didn't say anything, so I continued.

"When I got the call that she passed, I was shocked, and

after I got over that, my first thought was how this now changed my life trajectory. To be honest, it actually gave me a direction, something I needed to put my time and energy toward instead of wandering through life aimlessly, which I had been doing previously." I stopped rambling. For whatever reason, she was easy to share with.

"What about your family? Do you have any siblings?" I asked, attempting to turn the conversation to her.

"Nope, it's just me. My dad and mom separated when I was in middle school but have a relatively civil relationship now, so we get together for holidays and the occasional family dinner."

"And you live alone?"

"Yeah, I have a single bedroom apartment. Vi keeps trying to convince me to move in with her, but I don't want to have to drive that far for work every day."

"Maybe you can find a job closer to the city here?"

"Yeah, sure," she laughed. "You have no idea how long it took me to get where I'm at now. I don't particularly feel like starting over."

We fell into a comfortable silence, and I enjoyed watching her profile as she stared out at the passing city around us. We pulled up in front of my favorite Korean restaurant, and I stepped out and offered her my hand. As she followed me inside, I smiled in satisfaction at the looks we got as we walked through. She was breathtaking, and she was mine.

I really needed to figure out how to get her to move to the city, because I wasn't about to let her leave here and forget about me. Or if I couldn't convince her, I'd just have to buy a place close to her. We might not have known each other long, but I wasn't about to let her go now, I was obsessed.

I loved her body, yes, but it was more than that. Her tenacity, her smile that lit up the room, her infectious laugh, the way she mock glared at me, the way she actually did glare at me. She was a drug that I had only recently started using but couldn't go too long without now.

Our server led us to my usual table by the wall of windows overlooking the city.

"Art," she breathed. Another thing I loved. The way she said my name like it was a prayer.

I helped her into her seat and sat down across from her. "You like it?"

"It's beautiful." *Not as beautiful as you*, I wanted to say, but for some reason the words got stuck in my throat. Something about that seemed too personal right now.

We ordered our drinks, and I leaned back in my chair as she continued to take in our view. "Did you always want to be a journalist?"

"Pretty much. For as long as I can remember I've been writing little stories and news reports about both real events and ones I made up. Plus, my mom always told me I was way too nosey for my own good, but it turns out to be a helpful trait in this field."

I laughed as I pictured her as a little girl, scribbling away reporting fake events.

"I envy you."

"Me? What is it, the beat up old car I drive or the amount of times I've had a negative number in my bank account?" she asked with raised eyebrows.

"Definitely the beat up car. But no, seriously. The fact that you're passionate about something and pursued it with your whole heart."

"You have all the money in the world, you could pursue whatever you wanted to."

"That's the problem, I don't really have anything I want to pursue." *Except you.* Yep, I was definitely screwed.

"Well, then maybe it's time you discover your passions." She said it so matter of factly, and suddenly it sounded so easy.

"You should hang out with Finn, I think you'd get along."

"Your friend who invited me to the gala without your permission?" She laughed. "He definitely seemed like he wanted to hang out…"

"Scratch that, you're never seeing him again," I said as images of him flirting with her popped into my head and my fist involuntarily clenched.

"Hey, he got you to agree to take me to the gala even though you were clearly reluctant," she said on a laugh.

"I was not reluctant."

She quirked her eyebrow again in that way that I was growing to love. "Oh yeah, you definitely weren't gritting your teeth and planning my demise the whole time."

I reached across the table and took her hand in mine. "Okay, maybe I needed a little bit of encouragement to see past your desire to tear my company to shreds."

She winced, "I really didn't think it would bother you so much. From what I can tell, you should be used to people writing about you."

"Yes, well, I don't usually sleep with the people writing articles about me."

The prettiest pink tinged her cheeks as she ducked her head. "I'm going to tell Kim that I'm done here."

"Why?"

"Maybe I don't want to keep trying to find dirt on you to air to the public."

"Ava Schmidt, are you catching feelings for me?"

"Absolutely not," she said with a firm shake of her head.

I leaned forward and traced my hand down her arm as I watched her breath catch. "Liar," I whispered.

Our food arrived, and I sat back in my seat with a satisfied warmth in my chest. I wasn't the only one affected by our nearness, no matter what she said.

33

Ava

The date was amazing. I had been worried that the only thing we had was physical chemistry and we'd be stuck with awkward silences, but thankfully that wasn't the case. We took turns initiating conversation, and when there were silences, it was comfortable. I felt like I could be myself even though I was completely out of my element in the expensive restaurant.

We arrived back at the hotel, and I waved at Alonzo before heading inside. He'd driven me enough, even if I'd never spoken to him, that I felt like we should be friends.

Art followed me to the elevator, and I pressed the button for my floor. Once inside, he wrapped his arms around me from behind and I leaned into his warmth. I could definitely get used to this.

When we reached my floor, I expected him to continue upstairs, but instead he followed me to my door and pulled me into a hug.

"Thank you for tonight, I had a lot of fun." I said into his chest.

"I did too. Thanks for coming with me."

I leaned forward and pressed a quick kiss to his mouth before turning for the door. At his questioning look, I murmured, "No sex, remember?"

"Who said anything about sex?"

I raised my eyebrow at him as held his hands up in mock innocence. When I didn't back down, he groaned and leaned in toward me.

"Fine," he muttered. He pressed into me for a deeper kiss, and when I felt my back hit the door, he caged me in with his body. I involuntarily pressed my pelvis into his, and he pulled back enough to murmur against my lips, "You wanna reconsider?"

"No," I breathed back, trying to convince myself as much as him. I put a hand against his chest, and he immediately stopped. Honestly, his restraint was so incredibly attractive. It would make this so much more worth the wait.

"Goodnight, Art," I murmured before slipping inside my room. I waited at the door until I heard him walk away, then slipped off my shoes and headed for my bedroom but stopped in the doorway as I felt the hair on the back of my neck rise. Something wasn't right.

I looked around for what could have caused the feeling but didn't see anything out of the ordinary. I was tempted to call Art and make him come back, but what would I say? My room feels weird? Please check under my bed for me? There would be nothing to find, and then I really wouldn't have the courage to kick him out. I was just letting my overactive imagination run away with me.

I forced myself to enter my bathroom, remove my makeup and brush my teeth. By the time I slid into bed, I had convinced myself that I was just imagining whatever it was and I fell asleep hoping to dream of a six-foot man with dark hair and the prettiest blue eyes.

34

Art

I was in big trouble. Our date last night had been amazing, even if it only ended with a kiss. She was stunning, smart, and I loved hearing the way her brain worked and the things she was passionate about. I was falling for her, and I had no control over my own heart. But something about her made me want to lock her in my penthouse and never let her go.

I was still in bed reminiscing on the night before when I received a text from Jackson with a link. I didn't even bother reading his message before clicking on the article. An official statement from the New York police department.

Two dead at the Laurie hotel in New York City

On Monday June 7th, the New York police department were called to the Laurie for the murder of 63-year-old Drew Fulana. This marks the second suspicious death in the last week at the hotel. The investigation is ongoing, and at this time there is no reason to believe that these deaths are related. However, the police are using all resources to investigate and are requesting any information the public may have related to these deaths.

"Here we go," I muttered. I knew it was coming, but that didn't make it any easier. I sent off a quick text to Jackson confirming that I had seen the article and then called Ruby, asking her to come meet with me.

I was waiting for Ruby in my office when Tanya, our general manager, entered. She was young, probably not that much older than me, and usually had a friendly expression that welcomed questions and concerns. Today, she looked pale, with dark circles under her eyes. She took a seat across from me and got right to the point.

"I'm assuming you've seen the police statement."

"I have."

"Since they put that out, we have lost over half of our reservations."

I swore harshly under my breath. I had figured that the police statement would cause some public panic, but I hadn't expected it to be so severe or so soon.

"We need to get a press release out as soon as possible," she continued.

"I've already contacted Ruby, and she's on her way here to work on something," I told her. There was a moment of silence as we both sat processing.

"Over half?" I asked again, trying to wrap my mind around those numbers.

Tanya nodded. "We've never seen a cancellation like this before," she said quietly, "in any of the locations for any reason."

The statement was a punch to the gut. I knew I wasn't responsible, I wasn't the person murdering my guests, after all, but the fact that this had never happened under my mother's authority made me feel incredibly guilty. What was I doing wrong? How did I combat an enemy I didn't know?

I'd had my fair share of enemies over the years, I'd done some unsavory and illegal things, and I had no issues taking this into my own hands, but how could I do that when the police didn't even have any suspects?

The need to narrow down a suspect list overwhelmed me. Until we had something more to go on, we were stumbling along blind.

"We're doing what we can, trying to offer assurances and incentives, but people don't care. There's no reason to chance anything with us if they can go to a competitor and feel safer," Tanya said.

I rubbed my temples as I wracked my brain for anything I could do or say to help her, help my business. But I was coming up empty. Unless we stopped the murders, caught the person responsible, the public had no reason to resume their reservations. Thankfully this exodus was only affecting the New York location, but we would still need to start sending staff home if this didn't turn around soon.

Ruby arrived and was ushered into my office by Angie.

Tanya stood as she entered, and the women murmured brief greetings.

"Please keep me updated, Tanya," I said, before she left.

"Will do, boss."

"Arthur," Ruby said in greeting as she took Tanya's vacated seat.

"Ruby."

"It's been a hard week to be CEO," she remarked.

"You could say that again," I said, blowing out a breath. "I was told we are experiencing a mass exodus."

She nodded with a frown. "The police statement scared the public, I'm afraid."

"How do we ease those fears when we have nothing to offer them?"

"We can only try our best and hope they believe us. I've

written up a mock statement if you'd like to approve it before it goes public."

"Thanks. I trust you, but I would appreciate the chance to review it."

She slid over her laptop to display the message.

The New York police department issued a statement yesterday announcing the death of Drew Fulana, the owner of Knight Transportation. She was found deceased in her hotel room. So far, there is no reason to believe that there is a threat to the public; however, the safety of our guests remains our top priority. The Laurie is implementing several safety measures including increasing the number of security on staff and improving the security system, which affects individual room security, among other actions. The Laurie is committed to providing a safe, luxurious stay to every guest and is confident that we can continue to do so.

"Do you think it'll work?" I asked.

"Honestly? Only time will tell. But if I had to guess? No." She answered with a grimace. "I don't think anything is going to stop this mass hysteria until the killer is caught."

"I appreciate the honesty, but that's not at all what I wanted to hear from our head of marketing."

"I wish I had better news."

"Me too."

35

Ava

When I woke up the next morning it was with a smile still on my face from last night. I opted to order room service instead of heading downstairs for breakfast, then pulled out my computer and began going through my emails. While this was the main project I was on currently, I liked to keep up on other stories that were being covered and where I could go next. Especially since I had been serious last night when I told Art I wanted to be done with this story.

If I was honest, I was shocked that Kim still had me here. While, yes, the transition of ownership of the Laurie was news, plus a murder at the same time, still it really wasn't interesting enough to make sense that she wanted to keep me here. There were plenty of other stories to cover and investigate.

The thought of being done here was bittersweet. It would be nice to get back in the groove of writing and to stop tarnishing Art's name, but moving on most likely meant physically moving as well, and I had enjoyed the close proximity to Vi here, not to mention whatever was going on with Art.

I tried to put that out of my mind as I began looking through other stories being covered at the moment and things that I could pursue. I had just finished my breakfast when my phone rang. Art.

"Good morning," I answered with a smile.

"Hello, beautiful," the deep timber of his voice sent a shiver through me. "What are you up to today?" he continued.

I spun around in my chair as I answered. "It's Saturday, so I actually have a bit of time off since Kim hasn't given me any further assignments at the moment. What about you?"

"I was hoping I could see you today."

"Oh?"

"I thought maybe we could go to a museum or walk around a park if you were free."

"Well, that sounds romantic."

"I 'm offended that you sound so shocked by the thought."

I laughed. "Okay, maybe I'm a little surprised that you enjoy museums and parks on your days off."

"What can I say, I enjoy staring at beautiful things," he said in a husky tone.

"Has anyone ever told you that your pickup lines are nausea inducing?"

"Nope, I can't say that they have," he replied, and I could hear the smirk in his voice.

"Well, if you promise to dial it back, I'll let you take me out today," I conceded.

"Deal."

Half an hour later, I met Art in the foyer, where he brought me out to his waiting car.

"No Alanzo today?" I asked when he helped me into the front passenger's seat.

"Nope, I prefer to have you all to myself today."

My heart did a flip at his words. Whatever this had started off as, I could feel myself falling for him. His passion, his goofiness, his rare vulnerability. I wanted it all.

We spent the day exploring New York City and, despite the fact that I had been here many times before, it felt new seeing it with Arthur. Conversation flowed easily, and we somehow both ended up talking about our lives growing up, our passions, and dreams.

We ate lunch at a small restaurant in the city, and while Art used the bathroom, I took the opportunity to check my phone, which I'd stashed away all morning. The first thing I saw was an official statement from the New York police department announcing a second murder. My pulse sped up as I read. A serial killer? Here?

Art returned, and I showed him what I was reading.

"Did you know about this?"

His jaw ticked. "Yes, I spent the first several hours of my day talking with our head of security, general manager, and head of marketing trying to figure this out."

"I don't even know what to say."

"Join the club," he said as he took a long pull from his drink.

"I was shocked when Kim told me about the first murder, but two in a matter of a couple days?"

"Let me know if you find anyone who wants a hotel that's currently being used as someone's own personal murder grounds," he muttered in response.

I bumped his shoulder. "Hey now, they're going to catch whoever's doing this, and you'll be back to a full hotel full of celebrities and rich socialites soon."

He looked back at me with an eyebrow raised, looking wholly unconvinced. "I don't know where this optimism is coming from, but it scares me."

"I'll have you know that I'm a very optimistic person."

"That is not the vibe that I've gotten from our previous interactions."

"Have you ever considered that maybe that's a you problem?"

"Probably," he said with a smirk, and my chest warmed at seeing a glimpse of his playful side.

We finished lunch in peace and spent some more time walking the city before ending the day at a lakeside restaurant, where we walked and explored the gorgeous area.

"How did you meet Finn?" I asked as we strolled hand in hand in the fading light.

His answering laugh told me I was in for a good story.

"We'd both been sent off to boarding school, I was excited about the prospect of having freedom from prying eyes, and he was angry. We ended up sharing a room, and I snuck a tarantula into his suitcase. Side note, Finn is terrified of spiders."

I stopped walking and stared at him with an open mouth as he continued the story.

"Finn freaked out, then he beat me up when he figured out it was me. We ended up in detention together and decided we kind of enjoyed fist fighting each other, but from then on we mainly saved it for the boxing ring."

"You're serious."

"As a heart attack."

"I can't imagine Finn as an angry kid."

"Oh, he used to be nasty. But I mostly deserved it," he said with a chuckle.

"Of that, I have no doubt."

"Hey now," he said, elbowing me.

"Also, I'm scared to ask where you happened to just find a tarantula."

"It's actually not hard to get them," he started.

"If you ever even think about putting a tarantula in anything of mine," I interrupted him.

"I promise to never put a tarantula—"

"Or anything that resembles a spider."

"Or anything that resembles a spider anywhere near you," he said with a hand on his chest. "Scouts honor."

"You weren't a Cub Scout."

"Nope, but I still take the oath very seriously."

"You're ridiculous," I said with a laugh.

"Good, and that's how I know I'm doing my job properly," he said, tucking me against his side. I leaned into his warmth as a cool wind blew over us. Maybe things weren't so bad after all.

# # #

I woke Sunday morning feeling light. Yesterday had been pretty much perfect. Art had again complained that I wasn't spending the night with him, but I was serious about this. I wanted him for more than just something physical. I wanted to actually date him, which meant days like yesterday where we spent talking and getting to know each other instead of simply lying in bed. Not that I wasn't excited to do that again too.

My phone rang, and I looked down. It was Kim.

"Schmidt."

"Ava, I'm glad you actually picked up."

I tried not to let the comment bother me. Why she was acting like I was hard to track down was beyond me. "Of course."

"How is the story on Arthur going?"

"To be honest, I haven't found much more to add. I just saw the police statement as well as the announcement by the Laurie. I was unaware of the second murder, and I haven't

152

found anything more to add to that at the moment. When it comes to Arthur; frankly, I don't think the story is very interesting. I was going to tell you that I feel like I'm wrapped up here and was looking at where to head next."

"Good thing I don't pay you to feel."

Anger surged through me. No matter what I did, she always acted like I was an idiot who couldn't do a thing on her own. I'd been with this company for four years, I had done plenty to prove myself, and yet she always seemed like my current project would determine my value.

"Of course," I said again. "I'm just saying I think I could be better used somewhere else."

"I have another location for you to be," she continued as if I hadn't even spoken. "Tonight, I would like you to follow Arthur—."

I tuned her out as I tried not to let my irritation translate through the phone. Not only was I absolutely not interested in continuing this pointless story, but I wasn't going to go back on my word. I told Art I was done dragging his name through the dirt, and I meant it. Whether or not our relationship progressed, I valued my word. I wasn't going to keep doing this just to satisfy Kim's weird obsession with Arthur. *Definitely nothing to do with your developing feelings for him.*

"Sorry to interrupt you," I said when Kim stopped to take a breath. "I'm not interested in continuing to pursue this story. I was just looking and I saw the development in Lakewoods—"

"Are you refusing to follow my order?"

I swallowed and took a deep breath. "I'm not trying to refuse anything but—"

"But you won't continue this story and follow Arthur tonight?"

Nerves filled my stomach until it cramped, but I had to be

clear. "Yes, I'd rather head to Lakewoods—"

"No need."

I sucked in a breath at her cool tone and waited for her to continue.

"I'll send someone else to finish up out there. Effective today, you are no longer employed with the *Manhattan Press*. This week you have proven an inability to not only properly investigate and stay on top of a murder investigation but also show unwillingness to follow through with simple commands. Your room will be comped through this afternoon, and I expect your work equipment back by Tuesday."

Her words continued, but I stopped listening. Was she serious? I knew she'd be annoyed by my refusal to continue, but to fire me over this? Never would I have guessed that. After all these years. Why was she so invested in this?

"Any questions?"

Umm yes. Why? How? What the hell? "Not right now, no," I said instead.

"Good. I'll send over your official termination letter." With that, the call ended, and I was left alone with my shock.

36

Murderer

I cracked my neck as I stared at the video feed in front of me. The screen showed an empty hotel room where Ava should be. I had placed the camera in her room so that I could better track her and figure out my next move, but she spent the entire weekend gone with him instead.

I knew that they had had some interactions, but imagine my surprise when he asked her on a date, and they spent all day out with each other. They put up such a good show of hating one another when they were anywhere else.

I had originally planned on killing her next, bring the murders a little closer to home. But then I had seen that the security system had been revamped, and I wasn't confident in my ability to get back into her room unseen. So, then I figured I would lure her out to kill her, but now, after watching them together, I had other plans.

I had been waiting for this implosion for a long time. I wanted so badly to watch him crash and burn, but the other areas of my life were starting to close in on me, and I needed to get out fast. She might provide the perfect opportunity.

Instead of killing her off to try to sabotage the hotel, maybe I could use her as leverage to squeeze a large sum from Arthur. If I could get him to send me money in exchange for her, I could not only ruin him financially but also get my ticket out of here.

I had figured that a couple murders and bad press would send the business crashing and burning, but I'd underestimated his charisma with the investors. I also hadn't expected things in my personal life to accelerate so quickly either.

No matter. With enough money, I could start over somewhere new. I liked the sound of that better anyway, rather than staying in this shithole.

I closed the app and stood, walking to my worktable. A picture of Ava stared back at me, surrounded by information I had managed to gather on her.

"Enjoy your last day of freedom, Ms. Schmidt. Soon you will be my perfect ticket out of here."

Freedom and Art's destruction. I couldn't decide which one I would enjoy more.

37

Art

I felt like I was floating on a cloud. Even in the midst of murder investigations and the hotel revenue plummeting, I'd had the most amazing weekend. Ava made everything better, she could lift my mood just by a look. I kept expecting that as I spent more time with her the craving I felt toward her would lessen, but it only ever increased.

"You okay over there?" Finn asked from across the table, and I grunted in response. She also made it extremely hard to focus on anything else. I did, however, have a business to run, and one that was currently experiencing mass cancellations, which had not stopped.

I might not have been planning on becoming CEO so soon, but hell if I let something happen to the company. People already thought I was a failure, I wasn't going to prove them right.

"Yeah, sorry, just thinking."

The fact that he didn't come back with one of his usual snarky replies told me a lot about how much this situation was worrying him as well. He might not be high up in the police force or anywhere near a detective status, but he had a much better idea of these things than I did, and from what we could tell, NYPD had absolutely no leads and nothing to go on, despite the sketch they had gotten from the security guard.

"I just don't understand why. Maybe with the first one, the exec happened to be here when he was jumped and it was convenient. But two separate people with nothing to do with each other? Why make this specific hotel their hunting ground?" Finn wondered aloud.

I grunted again. I had absolutely no answer. I had all the money, all the connections and contacts, but what good was any of that in a situation like this?

"How did they get my credentials? And even with that, they have to have some connection to the security team. There's no way someone outside of the company would be able to get in and out of here like they have. Jackson swears they shouldn't be able to get around the security system like this. Both times, the cameras in the hallways have been spliced perfectly, leaving no trace." I said.

"So, it's someone on the security team," Finn mused.

"But why? And who? And how do we find them? There were different people on each night, no overlap," I responded.

"Could it be Jackson?"

I sat back in my chair and rubbed at my face. "I trust him, he has no reason to betray us like that. But I have no proof that it's NOT him. Except for the fact that he seemed just as surprised as us and has been working night and day trying to figure this out as well. It's his job, his reputation on the line, so I don't know why he'd do that. But I don't know a lot of anything these days."

"What you need is to loosen up," Finn remarked after a

moment of silence.

I snorted. "Why is that your answer to everything?"

"Because it works? Seriously, though, come out with me tonight. The boys and I are going out, and it would be a perfect opportunity to loosen you up."

"You mean it would be a perfect opportunity for me to pick up your tab."

He shrugged with a grin, "We aren't all made of money, Artie."

I had been hoping to meet up with Ava again tonight, maybe have her over to my place, but she hadn't responded to my texts yet today. She probably had some work to do, and if she wasn't free, I might as well go out with the guys. "Fine, when and where?"

# # #

I met the guys at a new nightclub that evening. Finn had invited several of his work buddies, including his roommate, Jake, who I'd hung out with on multiple occasions. I nodded at them as I took up the space next to them, and they all politely acknowledged me.

One of the drawbacks of having so much money was the strain it took on relationships. I had struggled to maintain any sort of real friendships for any length of time except for Finn. He loved my money, yes, but he had made it clear for years that he valued my friendship above just what I could do for him. That was really hard to find.

They were all talking work, and I enjoyed nursing my drink as I leaned against the booth and let them catch up. After a half hour or so of chitchat, our group was approached by a bottle girl. She smiled at us as she motioned behind her.

"Would you guys like a complimentary VIP room?"

The guys all began to murmur and elbow each other, and I

raised my eyebrow. What was the catch? She smiled shyly in my direction. "Someone noticed who we had here visiting, and we wanted to extend our welcome with hopes that you'll be back."

The guys were already following her, and I grabbed my drink and went with them. It was always bizarre to me how people like me with plenty of money were offered complimentary things when we were more than capable of paying for it. Regardless, the guys were excited, and I wouldn't turn down a private room, especially as the area around us got busier.

She brought us to an area in the back with plush benches and a glass table in the middle. I took a seat and watched her begin to fill up everyone's drinks. When she got to me, she opened a new bottle and smiled. "Mr. Michaels."

Something about the way she said it made my stomach turn. I nodded briefly, not wanting to encourage her, and she took the hint and moved on. Finn plopped down next to me.

"Not gonna lie, your status as Mr. Millionaire really comes in handy sometimes."

I grunted at him. "I'm so glad to be of use to you."

He laughed and threw an arm around me. "You know I'd hang out with you even if your presence never allowed us into another VIP section."

"That's the sweetest thing you've ever said."

He touched his chest, "I know, I'm the best."

I laughed at him and shoved him away from me. He bounced back with a gleam in his eye. "Thinking about how you're gonna bring Ms. Schmidt here?"

"I'm pretty sure I've told you that I don't like to hear her name in your mouth," I said as I took another swig of my drink.

He held up his hands in defense. "She's all yours, man, I just like to see you happy."

I raised my glass to clink it with his before taking another drink. My head was starting to feel fuzzy, but I hadn't drank nearly enough yet to be intoxicated.

I shook my head and set down my drink, waving over our bottle girl to ask for a water. She came back with one quickly, and I took a long guzzle. As much as I enjoyed the escape from reality that alcohol provided, I wasn't in the mood to be carried out of the club tonight.

Finn struck up a conversation with his buddy next to him about a recent case at work, and I leaned back against the cushioned back of the bench. I stirred when I felt a weight on me, and I pried my eyes open to find a scantily clad woman straddling me.

I attempted to move my arms to push her off me, but it felt like I was moving through mud and my limbs refused to obey me. What the hell was going on? She was grinding on me with her boobs pressed into my face, and her hands held my grip against her thonged ass. I tried again to move to no avail, and panic filled my body. Why couldn't I move?

"You okay there, buddy?" Finn's voice broke through my haze. I used all my strength to turn my head toward his direction, and while I couldn't get any words past my dry mouth, he must have seen the panic in my eyes, because he motioned to the woman sitting on me.

"Hey, I think he needs a minute." Thankfully, she removed herself from me and I tried again.

"Finn," I croaked out.

"Hey, we're gonna head out," he said to the guy next to him. He turned back to me. "Can you walk?" I again tried to make my arms follow my directions but nothing. He must have seen the struggle, because he called over someone.

"Hey, help me take Art out of here. How much did you drink, bud? I don't know if I've ever seen you this wasted."

I wanted so badly to respond, but I couldn't make it

happen. Finn and Jake practically carried me out and to the backseat of Jake's car, where I closed my eyes and only stirred again when the door opened, then Jake and Finn hauled me out and into the Laurie.

My limbs finally began moving, and I helped them get me into the penthouse, promptly collapsing into my bed. I heard Finn and Jake talking outside my bedroom, but I closed my eyes against the sound, desperately needing to sleep.

38

Ava

After getting fired yesterday, I took the rest of the day off and turned off my phone. Vi was busy with a shift, so I took the opportunity to wander the city. I avoided the spots that I had gone with Art and instead visited parts of the city that I'd never taken the opportunity to see before.

I should have left the Laurie already, since the company had stopped paying for my room, but the idea of having to find alternative housing was too overwhelming, so I reserved another night while I tried to figure out my next steps.

I had some savings, but not enough to keep me afloat unemployed for long. Where did I go from here? I wanted to talk it over with Vi, but she was busy. I wanted to talk to Art, but he was kind of the reason this was all happening in the first place. So, I spent the day wandering and thinking and trying to figure out my next steps.

The next morning, I woke up feeling no better with no clearer direction except for the fact that I'd need to check out today.

I turned my phone back on and automatically went to my favorite news site. I didn't even need to search anything because the first article I saw was a picture of Art at a club with his head slung back and a stripper straddling him. My stomach soured, and I immediately felt the need to vomit. What. The. Fuck.

New Company, Same Behavior

Millionaire playboy Arthur Michaels is back to his partying ways in the midst of plummeting profits and ongoing investigations. As the world watched to see how well he would take over his mother's company, is it a shock that he's still more invested in females than finances?

I looked for the author. Regina Andrews. Hadn't taken long for Kim to find my replacement. Is this what she would have sent me to do? Would he have done this had I been following him? Hell, why did he do it now? What about us? Was it all just a lie? Every pretty word he said, just an excuse to get me to sleep with him again? Wasn't it him who had mentioned not seeing other people? Did he think that it didn't count because she was a dancer?

Anger swirled in my gut. Betrayal coated my tongue, and I wanted to throw my phone across the room. Instead, I pulled up his contact with every intention of blocking and deleting and never thinking about him again.

Right before I pressed confirm, I paused. Maybe I was jumping to conclusions. Maybe there was an explanation. I wasn't a child, I could at least stick around long enough to hear him out.

I took several measured breaths before hitting call. With every ring, I felt my anxiety build. Was he currently passed out in someone else's bed? Did he have someone in his bed where I had been just a short time ago?

The call was finally sent to voicemail, and I spoke with a shaky breath.

"Hey, Art, Arthur. This is Ava. Anyway, I umm I saw an article this morning, and I'm just kind of confused. So, if you could, like call me back so we could talk. Yeah. Anyway, I'll talk to you later."

I ended the call and slumped back against the pillows. I was tempted to open the article back up to look at the picture, but instead, I threw my phone and closed my eyes against the rush of emotion. How had my life turned into this?

I let myself wallow in self-pity for a few minutes longer before I forced myself up and into the bathroom. After a scalding shower, shaved legs, and a hair mask, I was feeling a little more like myself, and I packed up the few things I had out before heading to the front desk.

I called Vi to leave her a message, intending to ask, or more like inform her, that I would be crashing at her place for the foreseeable future. When it rang to voicemail, I ended the call instead. I didn't want to try to explain myself over another answering service. I'd wait until she called me back. I had a key to her place anyway, so, worst case scenario, she came home to find me already camped out.

It didn't take long to check out of my room, and as I headed toward the front doors, my phone rang. My stomach dropped as I reached to see if it was Art. An unknown number. Could be a telemarketer. Could be someone from the *Manhattan Press* telling me they messed up and desperately wanted me back. I answered after several rings.

"Schmidt."

"Hello, Ms. Schmidt, this is Cain Mathews from the Laurie." I glanced around the lobby as if I'd see him here. Cain, the one who'd communicated with Kim and invited us here initially as well as attended that extremely awkward dinner with the four of us.

"Hi, how can I help you?" I answered.

"Sorry to bother you, I'm calling on behalf of Arthur." Arthur. Why was he trying to get ahold of me? And why ask Cain to be the middleman? Was he ashamed of what happened last night? Did Cain even know what happened? Not that Cain had any idea we had been together anyway.

Part of me wanted to just hang up and be done with it, but the part of me that had decided I was going to be mature about this insisted I hear him out.

"Is there something I can do for you or Mr. Michaels?" He must not have heard from Kim that I was no longer working here. Or that I had already checked out.

"He was hoping to meet with you today if you have time." Again, why couldn't he tell me this himself? But I couldn't really say that if Cain was unaware of our relationship. Or whatever it was we had.

"Well, you're in luck, my afternoon is free."

"Perfect, I can send a car down to pick you up."

"Oh, I'm actually already here at the Laurie."

"Unfortunately, Mr. Michaels is not there right now. Is it okay if you meet him for lunch instead?"

The longer this conversation lasted, the angrier I got, but I tried to push it down. "Sure, just tell me the place."

"Splendid, I'll text you the details." He hung up, and I settled into the foyer while I ordered a car and waited for his text to come through. When it did, I contemplated if I should bring my suitcase with me to lunch or drop it off at Vi's on the way. It was in the opposite direction, and I was now technically unemployed, so saving my money was probably the wise way to go. I would just have to tow it with me and let Art know it was goodbye.

The car took me toward a part of town that I wasn't familiar with, and all I could think of was how much this lunch was about to cost me. Maybe I could convince Art to pay for it. Maybe this whole thing truly was a misunderstanding.

Or maybe I was just delusional and naive.

The car turned into a car ramp for an industrial looking building, and I spoke up from the back.

"Umm, sorry, I don't think this is the right address. It should be a restaurant."

The female driver didn't say a word as she continued to drive, and panic filled my veins. What was happening? I pulled out my phone and immediately attempted to call Vi, but my phone refused to connect. I looked back up and watched the woman drive further and further underground.

"Hey, please let me out."

As the panic built, I reached for the door handle, but it refused to budge, and I could feel my heart rate speeding up with every passing second.

"I need to get out right now. I have someone waiting on me and they're going to know if I don't show up. They have my location tracker, and they'll be over here in no time."

The woman continued driving as if she couldn't even hear me. What was she doing? Why me? Where were we? How long until Art figured out something was wrong?

The part about him having my location was a lie that I had hoped would help, but no such luck. What did she want from me? I didn't have much money, but she could take anything I had on me. Was she someone connected to a previous disgruntled client? Why oh why hadn't I left a message for Vi telling her I was leaving? For all she knew, I was still at the hotel.

We finally parked, and she made no move to get out.

"Where are we?" I asked as my voice shook. Nothing.

Then, suddenly, my door opened, startling me and causing me to slam my knee on the console in an attempt to turn. A familiar looking man stood in front of me. Cain. Confusion rolled through me. Maybe I was in the right place? But why wouldn't she have just told me that?

"Hello, Ava. Thank you for joining us." Us. So, Art was here.

"Where are we?"

He chuckled lightly as the driver finally exited the car and pulled out my suitcase from the trunk. He didn't say anything else but offered me his hand. I didn't take it but used the moment to examine him. He was tall, taller than Art, and appeared to be in his late thirties or early forties if I had to guess. He had a clean shaven face and the start of some gray at his temples. His face was plain, nothing particularly remarkable about it, but his clothes dripped wealth. He wore an expensive looking watch and multiple rings. And something about the way he held himself made my hair stand on end.

"Please, Ms. Schmidt," he said, and his other hand came into view, holding a gun in an easy grip. I couldn't help the gasp that escaped, and I scooted back on the bench and pressed the button on my phone in an attempt to call the emergency line, but I could see that nothing happened.

"Why?" I croaked out. I looked toward my driver, but she was staring off in the distance, looking bored.

"Please, I'd prefer if I didn't have to hurt you," he said, motioning again for me to exit.

I didn't believe him. I knew in my gut I wasn't getting out unharmed. There was no way he had someone kidnap me if he was planning on being a gentleman. But there was nothing I could do here. No advantage I had. I needed to cooperate and try to remain levelheaded and find something that I could use to my advantage.

Slowly, I moved toward the open door and slid out without touching his outstretched hand. He chuckled again and immediately placed his free hand on the small of my

back as he motioned me toward the only door I could see.
"After you."

39

Art

I woke up to the worst headache of my life. I was intimately familiar with hangovers, but this was different. My throat felt thick and dry, my eyes burned when I tried to open them, and my stomach was cramping. After the third attempt, I finally got my eyes open and found myself in my bedroom. I attempted to sit up, but the world spun so fast that I immediately started retching and fell back onto my pillows.

"Easy," Finn's voice came from my side, and I didn't fight when he put a cool cloth on my head.

"What the fuck is going on," I managed to rasp out.

"I think you might have been drugged."

The words themselves were a surprise, but given the fact that my body felt like it had been put through a wood chipper, I wasn't all that shocked. All I could do was groan in response.

"Here, you should try to drink something."

I pried my eyes open and let him hold the bottle of water to my mouth. The cool beverage sliding down my throat felt heavenly. Had I ever tasted anything better than water?

"Easy," he said again as he pulled the bottle away.

I slumped back onto my pillow, and he set the bottle down next to my bed.

"How much do you remember from last night?"

I tried to make my brain work as I thought back to yesterday. "I remember talking about going to the club."

He nodded. "And?"

"And I don't really remember after that. Did we end up going?"

He pursed his lips. "We did, yeah. They gave us a complimentary room and bottle service, and you totally passed out after like one drink. I figured you must have pre-gamed or something, but when you seemed super agitated and out of it, we left."

"So, you think someone drugged me? Why? How"

He was uncharacteristically quiet for a long moment.

"Finn."

"You might want to check your phone." He handed me my phone, and I opened it to a news article already pulled up. The picture was a shot of me on the couch with a scantily clad blonde on my lap. The problem? It wasn't Ava. And I didn't remember it at all.

"What the fuck," I hissed.

I scanned the article, and it was the usual nonsense about me not giving a shit about the company et cetera. I looked at the author and realized it wasn't a name I was familiar with. I felt a moment of relief as I remembered Ava saying she was done writing shit about me. But that relief was short lived. "Ava!"

I pulled up my call log and found multiple missed calls and a voicemail from her. I listened to it and my heart sank with each word. I couldn't care less what the public thought of me. I had always had a bad public image. But Ava, did she really believe it?

Why wouldn't she? The picture looked pretty convincing. I mean, it was convincing, it had happened, even if I hadn't been conscious for it. I hit the call button and listened to my call ring to voicemail. I tried again but nothing.

"Hey, call me back please. We need to talk about the article. I—I can explain." I hung up and looked at Finn, who stood watching me. "I need to go downstairs. To her room."

He nodded. "You're in no state to be leaving your bed, let alone your room, but I can go get her and bring her up here. After you're a little more presentable."

"Go. Get. Her," I ground out.

He walked to my closet and came back with a pair of shorts and a t-shirt, which he threw at me.

"I'd suggest maybe brushing your teeth if you can manage your way to the bathroom." And then he was gone.

I pulled the clothes on and stumbled my way to the bathroom. By the time I made it there, I felt ready to pass out, so swishing mouthwash would have to do. I made it back to the bed without incident and collapsed into it. What if she refused to come? She wouldn't, would she? I'd just go break down her door if I needed to. Not that I'd need to since I owned the place and could just get security to open it for me.

By the time he returned, I had talked myself into going down myself, and seeing him come back alone just strengthened my resolve. As I attempted to stand, he put a hand up, "She's gone."

I stilled. "What do you mean she's gone?"

"She checked out this morning."

I glanced at my phone. "It's not even noon yet."

"Check-out is ten."

"Why would she check out today?"

Finn didn't bother answering. I tried her number again but nothing.

"You should eat something."

I nodded absently. I had no idea where she'd gone. She wasn't answering her phone, and for all I knew, she went back home since she was done here. I could easily find her address and head over there, but if I was going to do that, I should eat something and let my head transition from feeling like it was about to disconnect from my body. She might be pissed about the article, but if she thought she could run away and get me out of her life, she had another thing coming.

Finn left to get some food, and I gathered myself enough to wander out of the room and slid into the booth that took up a corner of the apartment. I had to admit, my mom had great taste when it came to furnishing and a living layout. I still wasn't used to seeing the place furnished with my stuff however.

Finn sat down across from me and placed a couple plates between us before pulling out his computer and starting it up.

"I've been thinking about the murders."

"And?" I asked as I attempted to eat a bite of toast.

"The fact that the security cameras have been tampered with, the rooms being accessed without difficulty, it has to be someone who has some reach here."

"Yeah, we already discussed it being an employee or someone with access to one."

"But it's not just any employee. I've been talking to Jackson, and you have a multiple verification setup required for access to any security related stuff. Except for a handful of people."

"Yes, but we know that someone stole my credentials to use, Sean saw them do it."

"Yes, but there's other parts of the system that need verification unrelated to your login."

"Okay…"

He pulled out a piece of paper. "This is the short list of people with the clearance needed to manipulate things if needed."

I glanced down. Short list indeed. Me, Cain, Jackson, Ruby, and Nathan.

"There's no way."

He raised his eyebrow.

"The COO, CTO, CMO, and CFO. Why would any of these people be murdering guests in our hotel?" I went on. "Plus, we have the sketch of the guy who broke into the security room, and it wasn't one of them."

"I didn't say they were the ones doing the murdering. But if they wanted to, they could tamper with anything in the organization. And one of them could have easily hired that guy to come in."

"But why would they want the hotel to fail? And why now? They've been with the company since my mom started it practically."

"Not sure. Blackmail maybe? Either way, I think it's our best lead."

"Why haven't the detectives pursued this? What are we going to find that they haven't?"

"They could very well already be working this angle. I'm not privy to what they have going on, so this is the best that I could come up with on my own."

I let that sink in. Was it possible? Was someone in my organization murdering people or at least aiding? How long had this been going on and I was oblivious? I needed to get ahold of Ava, but maybe I also needed to help Finn with his.

"Okay, where do you want to start?"

"I think we should do some digging into their personal lives. See if there's any area where they could be getting blackmailed or something that rings alarm bells."

"Done," I said, pulling up my phone to text for the second time this week.

I had met Toni in boarding school, when we were both placed in detention, me for something stupid, her because she had hacked into one of the teacher's accounts. We'd become friends and I discovered that there wasn't much this computer geek couldn't do. I had always figured I would need her services for one thing or another, but I was very quickly becoming indebted to her.

I didn't care, if she helped me solve these murders she would have a permanent place on my team. Honestly, with how she had helped me with Mark she already had one.

Regardless, it wouldn't take long for her to get a comprehensive history and information on my team. If there was something to be found, she would find it.

# # #

Hours later, and we were still at the breakfast nook going through information. Toni had delivered like I knew she would, and Finn and I were dividing and conquering the list. Finn had insisted on starting with Jackson, as he was the most "obvious" choice as chief technology officer. He hadn't found anything noteworthy (honestly did the guy even have a life outside this job?), and now he'd moved on to Cain. I was taking Ruby and Nathan, as they were the people I had the least interaction with.

Ruby was a single mom to two adult children. She had been with my mom for years, and as chief marketing officer she'd done an excellent job with the company. One of her kids was married with a couple young children, the other might have some gambling problems, but nothing about her finances showed that she was in dire need of money to the point of blackmail. And how would ruining the company image help with money problems anyway?

I rubbed at my temples and took another large swig of water. The ibuprofen I'd been popping helped ease the headaches, but I still felt like shit. That was another thing. Was the fact that I was drugged related to the murders? And how?

"That's interesting."

I looked over at Finn. "What?"

"Do you know much about your mom's romantic interests?"

"Nope, and I plan to keep it that way."

"Sorry, but not anymore. Did you know she was sleeping with Cain?"

"She was what? Like Cain Mathews?"

"The one and only."

"Well, that's disgusting. He's what, fifteen years younger than her?"

"And married."

My eyebrows rose at this. "I've never heard him talk about his wife. Or partner, or whatever."

"Not surprised given his extracurriculars with your mom."

"Anything else you find so far?"

"Nope, that's about it."

"Well, on that note, I'm going to take a break and go vomit. Thanks for that," I said, pushing up from the table and heading toward my room. The effects from last night were still lingering. Once I figured out who'd drugged me and why, I was going to pay them a nice little visit.

40

Ava

Cain took me up several flights of stairs and into a large open room that looked like it had previously been an office building. It was bare now and covered in dust, but there were several windows letting light stream into the space. I looked around for anything I could use as a weapon or a way to escape, but the only exit appeared to be the door we had come through. Cain motioned for me to follow him, and I didn't have much choice with the gun still in his hand.

"Where are we?"

He didn't answer.

"What are we doing here?"

He opened a door and motioned me inside what appeared to be a small closet with empty shelves. I stopped before entering, having the distinct impression that if I went in I might never come out alive.

"Why am I here?" I tried again.

Cain finally looked at me. "Leverage."

"Leverage?"

"Arthur has something I want, and I think you may be the best way to get it."

"How?"

"I really don't feel like explaining myself to you," he said as he motioned with the gun for me to enter the closet. I swallowed and looked around frantically, but there was no reason to stall any longer. I had no upper hand here.

"I need to use the bathroom."

He stared down at me and put the gun against my back. I stiffened as I felt the cold metal through my shirt.

"Please get inside."

I entered without another word and shivered when the door slammed shut and locked with a distinct click, then his steps retreated, and I let my eyes adjust to my new space. The light coming in from under the door allowed me to see a little in the closet. It truly was empty. The only thing in here was cracked white shelves and dust.

I tested the shelf closest to me but it didn't budge, then reached up for the second shelf and felt it creak beneath my grasp. I paused to listen for any noise from outside the closet but heard nothing. I grabbed the shelf again and yanked hard, loosening the wood from the wall. With a couple more pulls, it came away in a cloud of dust. I stopped to listen again, but either Cain had left or didn't care about the noise I was making in here.

I looked down at the board at my feet. I could possibly use it as a weapon to hit Cain or whoever else came for me, but with his gun, it wouldn't do much good. Even still, it made me feel a little better. More than a weapon, however, I needed something to help me get out of here.

I looked again at the wall and noticed that when I had ripped off the shelf, I had left behind some nails that were still buried in the wall. I reached up to feel them. They were stuck deep. It was not going to be easy to get them out of there.

I gritted my teeth and ran my finger over them until I found the one that was sticking out the furthest. I dug my fingernail under the head of the nail, attempting to dig it out. It didn't budge. I tried again, and searing pain shot through my fingertip as my fingernail ripped in half at the cuticle.

"Fuck!" I swore as I stuck the throbbing finger into my mouth and bounced from one foot to the other. After several moments, I ran my hand along the wall again. The nail hadn't even moved. I felt tears burn behind my eyes in frustration. I could do this. I had to.

I tried again with another finger and felt the nail shift under my touch. I adjusted my grip and pulled. The nail broke free just as I felt my second fingernail rip. This time the tears fell freely, and I tried to stifle my cries as my finger burned with the pain. Blood oozed out from where my nail tore from my finger, and I stuck that finger in my mouth as well in an effort to soothe the burn.

When I finally felt more in control, I walked over to the door and attempted to stick the nail into the lock. After some maneuvering, it slid into the bottom of the knob, and I twisted and turned, but nothing happened.

I tried to keep my emotions in check and not let myself sob in frustration. I'd never picked a lock before, but I knew from watching movies that there were multiple parts to a lock that you needed to hit in order to unlock it. I stopped and tried to think. I needed something small like a safety pin, bobby pin

Bobby pin! I ran my hands through my hair, but I hadn't done my hair this morning in my packing and checking out of the hotel. I reached into my jean pocket as I sent up a quick prayer, *Please, oh please.*

I felt something cold against my finger, another tear slipping free when I realized that my prayer had been answered. I pulled out the small piece and promised myself I'd never leave the house without a bobby pin again. That's if I ever got out of this. No, I couldn't think like that.

I opened the pin wide and stuck an end in my mouth to peel off the rubber casing. I approached the door again and took a steadying breath. I could do this. There was no other option. I placed the bobby pin in the top of the hole and the nail in the bottom. I began jiggling them in an attempt to feel any sort of click and give. After much trial and error, I heard a soft click and felt a release. Had I really done it?

I held my breath as I took my makeshift lockpick set out and tried to turn the knob. It turned and the door swung open. I half expected Cain to be standing on the other side grinning, but he wasn't. The room was empty.

I debated closing myself back in the closet and waiting until it got dark so that I had a better chance of sneaking out, but I had no idea where Cain had gone and no idea when he'd be back or if he planned to kill me when he did. No. I had to leave now.

I stuck my bobby pin and nail in my pocket and stepped out of the closet, attempting to keep my steps silent on the wood floor. I crossed the empty room without an issue and reached the door we had used to enter. I took another shaky breath before trying the handle. It opened without difficulty, and I looked out into an empty hallway.

Fear tightened my stomach and made my legs shake, but I had to push through. I knew which way we'd come from the garage, and as much as I hated the thought of going back there, I couldn't chance heading in the opposite direction when I had no idea where it led. So instead, I took a right and started toward the stairwell. I opened that door and entered. We'd parked in an underground parking ramp, but there was a good chance that the stairs would have an access door on the main level I could leave through instead. I didn't know what kind of building this was, except that it seemed abandoned.

I started down the stairs and heard each step echo as I went. There was no way I was going to be quiet, so I went for speed instead. I had made it down one flight of stairs before I heard a door above me open. I froze and heard footsteps slap on the stairs as if someone was running. He'd found me gone.

Terror filled my veins, and I took off, racing down the steps, ignoring the dizziness that gathered as I turned in circles down and down. The sound came closer, and I began to pant as I tried to push my legs as fast as they'd go. I had to be approaching the bottom. I had to be close, and then I'd push through the door, I'd get out into the open where someone could see me and—

I felt something firm against my back, and then I was falling forward. I caught myself with my outstretched hands before my head slammed into the floor, and I tumbled down the rest of the concrete steps and hit the wall at the bottom. My scream was ripped from my mouth as I lost my breath from the impact, and pain ricocheted through my skull when I attempted to open my eyes.

"Bitch," I heard above me before I felt rough hands grip my shoulders and lift me. I cried out as every nerve ending in my body seemed to scream in agony. I opened my eyes to meet Cain's fuming gaze.

"Let me go," I whimpered.

"Not a fucking chance, sweetheart." He threw me over his shoulder, and I cried out again as my bruised body bounced against his. He began the trek back up the stairs, and I let the tears fall. I had failed.

41

Art

We had spent the day looking through files and after an afternoon of searching had really only discovered that Cain was an unfaithful creep and Nathan liked to drink and drive. We called it quits earlier than we probably would have thanks to my lingering headache and agreed that I would pick back up tomorrow, while Finn went to work.

The next morning, I woke up headache-free and celebrated this blissful sensation with a large espresso. Finn had slept over in one of my guest rooms and was still getting ready for work when I heard a knock on my front door. Angie came forward to answer it, but I waved her off from my spot at the table. I made it to the door, curious who was visiting this early in the morning, and came face to face with Victoria, Ava's friend from the club.

"Hey," I said, letting her into my place as my heart began to pound. Had something happened to Ava? Had she said something about me? Had she sent her friend over? Why?

"Hey, I'm Victoria, I don't know if you remember me, but

I'm Ava's best friend, and we met at the club a week ago."

"I remember you, yeah. What's up? Is Ava okay?" I said, cutting to the chase.

"That's actually why I'm here. I'm not sure."

"What do you mean?"

I haven't heard from her in a couple days—" her sentence cut off as Finn came into the room.

"Beour," he murmured from the other side of the room. I ignored him as I forced her attention back to me.

"What do you mean you haven't heard from her?"

"She called me yesterday while I was at work, but when I tried to call her back, she didn't answer, which isn't like her. I mean, sometimes she's busy, but she always calls me back. So I came over here to check on her and make sure she was okay, but the front desk won't tell me what room is hers. So I came up here."

"She checked out yesterday," I said when she finished talking.

"What?" she said as surprise colored her face. "Why? She didn't tell me."

I had figured she didn't tell me because of the article. But the fact that she hadn't told Victoria either didn't sit right with me, and the panic from before came back in full force.

"That's something I'd love to know." I called Jackson, and he answered on the first ring.

"I need footage of the hallway outside room 2307 as well as the lobby from yesterday."

"On it. Has there been another murder?" he questioned.

I wanted to strangle him for asking such a question, as if by him voicing it, it was going to make that a reality. But that was stupid. She had left of her own volition. She was probably just mad about the club picture. But why hadn't she told Victoria she was leaving? Her friend was clearly worried.

"Just get it to me."

"On it, boss."

I hung up and turned toward Finn and Victoria. "Did she go back home?"

"She wouldn't have without talking to me first. There's no way," Victoria replied, shaking her head.

"Jackson is getting security footage from yesterday. He'll come meet us," I said, starting to pace.

Something was wrong. I didn't know what, but it was. Why would she have checked out without talking to me or Victoria? I didn't usually consider myself a paranoid person, but with the recent murders here, it was hard to keep the panic at bay. She had to be okay. We'd find her, and she would be fine.

# # #

"There's not much," Jackson said in way of greeting. He set the laptop down with footage pulled up from the lobby yesterday morning. We gathered around the table and watched as Ava chatted with the front desk before heading toward the door. She paused as she answered a call on her phone and then glanced around the lobby. After a brief conversation, she ended the call and settled into a seat. She continued to stare at her phone for a while longer before heading outside.

Jackson typed into his computer for a second before new footage pulled up. Ava left the hotel with her suitcase in tow and headed toward a car that was parked out front. She chatted with the female who got out and helped her put the suitcase into the trunk. Then she slid into the backseat, and the car left.

"That's all there is."

"Rewind it so I can get the license plate."

Jackson did so without a word.

"Who was she on the phone with? I'm going to call her parents and Kim," Victoria said as she left the room.

I wrote down the license plate and headed to my own room to make my own calls. This might be an overreaction, and there was a chance that she had simply gone back home, but something told me Ava was in trouble, and I was going to use every resource I had to find her.

42

Ava

I awoke to the taste of blood. I attempted to open my eyes but one was swollen shut and my head ached. I tried again and saw nothing in the darkness around me. I struggled to move my arms and push myself off of my side but found them secured in front of me with something that felt like rope. I tried again, but nausea rolled through me, and every single part of my body ached. Tears slipped down my face, and I finally gave up trying to move as I just let myself cry as my thoughts swirled.

Why had he taken me? What did he want from Arthur that he was using me as leverage for? Was he going to kill me? Why hadn't he done it yet? Was he responsible for the other murders in the hotel?

I heard the sound of a door opening, then multiple pairs of footsteps outside my door, and I braced myself for whatever was about to happen, but they didn't enter my space, which I finally realized was my previous closet again.

"I just don't know why you haven't gotten the money yet,"

came a familiar feminine voice from the other side of the door.

"Which is exactly why you aren't calling the shots here," Cain sneered in response.

"The longer you wait, the more likely they're gonna figure it out," she argued in return.

"It's been twenty-four hours, calm down."

"That's twenty three hours longer than I'd like to be here."

"If you're so worried, then leave."

"You promised me cash—

"Which I will give you as soon as he sends it. Now leave if you're going to continue to whine so I can actually do something."

Footsteps echoed as she left the room, and I closed my eye again. Was he expecting money from Arthur? What did I have to do with any of this?

My head was spinning, and it was hard to concentrate on a particular train of thought. I was sure I had a concussion, and I desperately needed to pee. No one knew I was here. No one knew I had left to meet Art and Cain. Art. I hadn't said anything in my last voicemail to indicate that I was leaving. What was he going to think when he found out that I checked out? He'd probably think that I went back home. Had Cain told him he had me in exchange for money?

And Vi. Why hadn't I left a voicemail or at least texted her that I was going to lunch? She didn't even know that I had checked out of the hotel.

Fresh tears poured down my face, which just made everything hurt worse. I couldn't even get myself to a seated position let alone get out of here. I had no hope of escaping again and no one knew where I was or had any indication that anything was wrong.

I was helpless and stuck waiting for Cain to implement whatever plan he had in mind. I could only hope that if he hadn't killed me yet, he wasn't going to. But there was no way he'd let me leave alive knowing who he was, right?

Desperation, pain, and panic filled my veins as I laid on the floor and cried.

43

Art

Every second that I waited for more information felt like an eternity. I had passed the vehicle information on to Toni, and she was able to trace it to a woman named Sarah, who worked for a taxi service, and that's where the trail ended. Toni was pulling up everything she could find on her, while Victoria was making her own calls.

"She fucking got fired!" Victoria yelled, pulling me from my phone.

"She what?"

"I tried to get ahold of her old company to see if she had been sent on a different story or something, but they said she's no longer employed there."

"Since when?"

"It's news to me, she didn't say anything when we last talked."

"I haven't talked to her since our date, but she told me she was going to tell Kim she was done writing about—well, me."

189

"And that bitch fired her over it? I knew I hated her."

"So, if she got fired, where did she go?" Finn chimed in.

"Her parents haven't heard from her. She's not picking up, but maybe she went back to her apartment and is just hiding out."

"Then let's go," I said, grabbing my keys and wallet. Victoria chewed on her lower lip and then nodded.

"I have a key to her place, so we can check it out. I just hate the idea of heading further away from here if she's not there."

"Toni is still looking into Sarah's information," I said.

"We need to figure out who she was talking to before she left," Finn stated. I nodded as I typed out another message to Toni.

"On it, now let's go check out her apartment."

We all piled into my charger, and Victoria typed Ava's address into my phone. It was an hour and a half drive to her apartment, and twenty minutes into the drive, my navigation was interrupted by an unknown number. On the off chance that it was Toni from a different number, I answered.

"Michaels."

"I have your girlfriend," came a robotic voice.

I slammed on the breaks, causing my tires to squeal and the car behind us to swerve as it barely managed to avoid rear-ending us.

"Fecking hell!" Finn yelled from the back seat.

"Where. Is. She," I ground out as Victoria gasped and covered her mouth.

"One million dollars by midnight tonight or she dies."

I looked into the rearview mirror, and Finn was already typing into his phone.

"If you fucking touch her—"

"One million. I will text you the details."

"I'm not sending you shit until I know she's okay."

"I will send you proof of life—"

"Proof of life? Proof of fucking life?!" I yelled as my voice cracked.

The call ended, and I slammed my fist against the wheel as a car behind me honked.

"Pull off the road, man. Pull over before someone hits us and call Toni."

Fury rippled through me as the realization hit me. She had been taken because of me. They were trying to get to me, get fucking money out of me.

Persistent honking pulled me out of my tirade, and I slammed on the gas and drove until I reached the next exit, while pulling up Toni's contact.

"They're coming after me," I said when she answered. "I just got a call from someone, I need you to trace their number. They're sending me information, they want me to transfer a million dollars. I'll do it, whatever they want, but you have to fucking find her."

"Send it to me. I'll find her."

"I need to do something."

"Send me the information. I'll let you know as soon as I have something," she said again before ending the call. I ground my teeth so hard that my jaw ached.

"We need to go back to our hunt. This has to be related to the murders, the security compromise. It's way too much of a coincidence. We need to figure out which one of them is at least involved in this," Finn said from the back seat.

I nodded as I spun the car around and sped back to the hotel.

"Do you have that kind of money?" Victoria asked quietly from beside me.

"What?"

"Did you mean it when you said you'd transfer the money for her?" She asked.

"Yes," I answered without hesitation. "I will do whatever I

need to, sell whatever parts of the company, I will get the money if that's what it takes to get her back."

She nodded wordlessly and I was thankful she didn't press me more. It was just money. If I needed to drain my account or sell the company, I'd do it. She had been taken because of me. Someone had gone after her because of her association with me and I would destroy anything including my mother's company if that's what it took to get her back.

We made it back without getting pulled over by some miracle. Maybe Finn had a sign he was waving out the window saying *'I'm with him, leave us alone.'* Whatever the reason, we were soon huddled around the computer in my office, Finn seated in a chair next to me and Victoria pacing in front of the desk.

"It can't be Jackson, there's no way," I said, staring at the information we had gathered before us.

"I agree, I don't think it's him either. But why would it be one of the other three? We need to find their motive."

My stare flitted from the computer screen to the paper on the desk. Unhappy man cheating on his wife, invested mother of a gambling addict, older man who liked to drive drunk and seemed to be deeply invested in his religious organization.

"I just keep coming back to your mom," Finn finally spoke up from where he was scrolling on my computer.

"What do you mean?"

"Her and Cain were hooking up. Why? For how long? Something about that doesn't sit right with me."

"I mean it's gross, but what does that have to do with Ava?"

"Nothing, but it has a lot to do with you."

"I guess I could look through some of her old papers. There's still quite a bit that were boxed up from in here and just moved to a storage closet down the hall."

Finn followed as I led the way to the closet, and it didn't take long until we had everything moved back into the office. Victoria stopped her pacing long enough to come watch us as we started through the papers. We worked in silence for a while before I paused on the letter I was holding.

"Didn't you say Cain was still married?"

"Yeah, he has a wife and a couple kids. Why?"

"I found a letter from him to her talking about how they're going to get married and move in together."

"What?" Finn leaned in to read over my shoulder. "Well, that's even weirder than just hooking up. I had no idea they were that serious."

"Neither did I. My mom and I weren't close, but I feel like she would have mentioned it if she was literally about to marry the guy."

"Maybe they weren't."

Finn and I both glanced back at Victoria, and I felt a moment of guilt, as I had all but forgotten she was here.

"What do you mean?" Finn asked before I could.

"Your mom was super wealthy, right?" she asked me.

"I mean, yes, the Laurie is doing very well."

"And she was planning on passing the company on to you someday."

"Not anytime soon, but yes, eventually."

"So, Cain was never going to own it."

"I mean, he basically owns it, he's the COO."

She shook her head. "It's not the same."

"No, she's right," Finn noted from beside me, and I had to try to stop myself from rolling my eyes. Even with all that was going on, I'd noticed the way he looked at her. His automatic agreement with her just solidified that.

"If Cain was sleeping with your mom, maybe he felt entitled to more of the company than he was getting."

"Okay, but it's a large jump from sleeping with my mom to

murdering guests in the hotel, don't you think?"

Finn shrugged. "Money is one of the biggest motivations for murder."

"Okay, say he was capable of murder. What does killing people in the hotel get him? And why take Ava?"

Just saying those words aloud made my stomach roil, and I wanted to vomit or scream or break something. Who knew what was happening to her while we were sitting here chasing our tails.

"I'm not sure, but I think getting ahold of him would be a good start."

Just then, my phone rang, and I answered before the second ring. "Toni."

"I found her," she said breathlessly.

"Ava?!"

"Fuck, no, I'm sorry. I found Sarah."

44

Art

"Where is she?" I demanded.

"I'm sending the location to your phone right now."

As if on cue, my phone buzzed with a notification.

"It's a single family home, and from everything I can tell, she's there right now."

I was already up and out of my chair, heading for the door. Finn and Victoria were close on my heels, and I hung up on Toni with a thanks.

"You're not coming."

"She's my best friend," Victoria argued.

"I'm not letting you go alone," Finn added, both of them talking over each other.

"You're not coming," I said again and put my hand up before they could argue further. "I need you to keep digging to see what you can find, something beyond speculation. I'm going to go talk to this Sarah, and believe me, you are not going to want to be around for it."

This caused Finn to pause, but Victoria continued on,

undeterred.

"If you have her address, call 911, we need everybody over there, maybe she's there right now, we need to get to her."

I put my hand on her shoulder and gave it a gentle squeeze. "I know you don't know me or have any reason to trust me," I said as she stared at me unblinking. "But I swear to you, I will do everything in my power, legal and illegal, right or wrong. I will do whatever it takes to get Ava back, and when I do, you will be the first person I call."

She continued to stare at me before giving the tiniest nod. "Save her."

And with that, I was gone.

I called Toni as soon as I was in my car and almost cried in relief when she told me that she had not seen Sarah leave her house.

"I sent someone there, so if for some reason she leaves before you get there, she'll have a tail. She won't get far," she reassured me.

"Remind me after this to get you whatever you want."

"Oh, I'm counting on it, Michaels," she said with a dry laugh. "From everything I can see, her only source of income is driving. Financially, she seems to be barely getting by, but let's be real; who isn't these days." A pause. "Don't answer that, I know you're shitting Benjamins."

"So, you're telling me this could just be a wrong place at the wrong time situation."

"Could be," she said noncommittally.

"I'll call you if I need you," I said in lieu of goodbye.

"I'll be watching," she said before hanging up. I didn't even want to ask what that meant.

I arrived in front of a two-story building that had clearly seen better days. The grass was too long, the paint chipping, and the sidewalk cracked. I took in the nearby neighbors and sent off a quick text to Toni. *I might need the neighborhood evacuated.*

On it, came her reply less than a minute later.

I cracked my neck and headed for the front door, where I knocked and put on my best attempt at a smile. *She might be innocent. She might have nothing to do with this,* I kept reminding myself as I waited. After several moments, a dog barked, and she opened the door.

"Can I help you?" she asked suspiciously.

"Yeah, I was hoping to come in and chat about a friend of mine who's missing," I said, straight to the point.

Surprise flashed in her gaze, and I used her shock to push my way in, closing the door behind me in one motion. Before she could turn and bolt, I pulled out my Glock and waved it in her direction. She stumbled backwards and landed on her couch.

"I just want to talk," I said, although that wasn't entirely true. She looked between my face and my gun, and I could see her mind racing. "If you cooperate, I'll let you go," I said, again lying but needing her to go along with this.

I could tell she didn't believe me, and she took a deep breath, but right before I assumed she was about to let out a screech, a loud siren pierced the air as the tornado siren began to blare throughout the neighborhood.

I sent a mental thanks to Toni as I tucked my Glock in my waistband and used the opportunity to yank her off the couch and throw her over my shoulder. She kicked at me, but I got an arm around her knees, pinning her in place. She began to pound and claw at my back, and I gritted my teeth as I felt her nails scratch me through the material. She might be half my size, but the panic that fueled her gave her a good fight.

Toni had sent over the layout of the house, and I'd memorized it on my way over. She had a basement which would have to do for now. The siren continued blaring, and with any luck, it would not only drown out any noise but also maybe cause people to evacuate.

I kicked the door open and carried a squirming, screaming Sarah down the steps into her basement. It was unfinished, and I almost tripped down the steps. Once I reached the bottom and deposited her on the concrete floor, she hit the ground hard and her breath came out in a cry.

"Where. Is. Ava." I said, looking down at where she lay on the floor.

"Go to hell."

"Real original."

She continued to glare at me, and I stared right back. "Where did you take her?"

"You're not going to find her."

"I just can't figure out what you're getting out of it," I said as I reached back and pulled out my Glock again. Her eyes went wide at the sight as I took another step toward her.

"What are you going to do?" she said as she attempted to crawl away from me.

"See, here's the thing. That woman you took in your car? She's very important to me. And while I don't appreciate anyone being taken against their will, present company excluded, I *really* don't like the fact that you fucked with my girl. So, I'm counting on the fact that you have even an ounce of self-preservation and care more about your pathetic life than whatever you were promised."

"I don't know his name, but he had me take her to a warehouse in the middle of the city," her words tumbled all over themselves in an attempt to get out.

"Where?"

"I don't know the address off of the top of my head, but I can get it for you!" she stammered as I stepped closer and pressed the barrel of the gun against her head.

"What did he look like?"

"He's tall with graying hair," she whimpered.

Fuck.

"Why?"

Her panicked voice was now interrupted by sobs as she began to cry. "I don't know, he promised me money if I would help bring her over there. He didn't tell me why, he just promised me money, my mom is sick, I can't afford her chemotherapy treatment, please, you have to believe me," she cried hysterically.

"Address, now."

"It's on my phone, I'll get it for you, just let me go, please."

I kept my gun trained on her as I gave a sharp nod. She dug into her pocket and pulled out her phone while I pressed the gun against her temple again. She shook violently as she scrolled through her texts messages until she pulled up an address. I reached down and plucked the phone out of her hand before stepping back from her. She cowered before me, and I shook my head in disgust. She was pathetic. Not even worth another moment's consideration.

I turned to leave her in the basement, when I thought back to the image of Ava trusting her as she willingly slipped into her car. I take that back, maybe she was worth a second more.

I spun around and shot Sarah in her right foot. The sound echoed through the basement, causing my ears to ring and Sarah to begin screaming in pain.

"That's a parting reminder for every time you drive a car in the future." And then I left.

I called Toni on my way to my car to tell her she could stop the siren and to give her the address.

"That's in the other direction from where you are."

"Is Finn closer at the Laurie?"

"Yes."

"It's Cain, she gave me a description. I need you to find him if he's not there."

"I will," she said with certainty.

I hung up and called Finn.

"Yes," he answered on the first ring.

"We have an address. You're closer, I need you to head that way in case you get there before I do."

"Do you want me to call it in?"

"No. I don't know if he has someone paid on the force, I don't want to spook him."

"Okay," I could hear the reluctance in his voice.

"And, Finn." A pause. "If you get to her before I do—"

"I promise, I'll do everything in my power to keep her safe." I believed him. I knew he'd do that for her no matter what she meant to me. But still, the thought of someone else getting to her first made me press my foot harder onto the accelerator.

"Hurry."

45

Ava

I awoke to the sound of a door nearby and footsteps getting closer. It took all of my concentration to open my good eye and roll to my back, the movement causing my stomach to heave, but nothing came up. I had no idea how long I had been out, but based on the light coming through the bottom of the door, I thought it was still daylight, though I couldn't be sure.

My stomach was aching but nauseated, I was covered in my own piss, and I could feel blood on my face from where it had run down and dried. But it wasn't actively bleeding, so that was something.

I didn't think I'd broken any bones in the fall, but my head wouldn't stop spinning enough for me to really take inventory of my body. And my stupid broken nails were still throbbing.

I heard the steps move closer, and I held my breath. Cain hadn't been back for some time now, but I was terrified that he had decided to finally come finish the job. Something scratched against the closet door, and I couldn't help the whimper that escaped. It didn't matter to be quiet anyway, since it wasn't like Cain didn't already know where I was.

The door finally opened, and I blinked at the sudden blinding light.

"Fecking hell," came from above me as I attempted to focus my one eye. My vision was blurry, but I saw a masculine face surrounded by a mop of orange curls. My heart began racing as I realized that it wasn't Cain and maybe someone had finally come to save me.

"Help me," I managed to croak out, and the figure dropped to his knees in front of me.

"Ava, my god." He knew me. I tried harder to focus.

"Finn?"

"Yes, Finn, good job," he said encouragingly as if I were a small child.

"How?" I wanted to ask how he found me, but the rest of the words got stuck in my dry throat.

"I'll explain everything, but right now we need to get you out. Do you know where Cain is?"

I shook my head, which I knew instantly was a mistake when my body involuntarily began to retch.

"Easy, easy," he murmured as he gently rubbed my shoulder. When my stomach calmed, he reached down and pulled out a knife that he used to cut the ropes binding my wrists. I whimpered as my hands began to tingle from the rush of blood.

"I'm sorry," he said with a wince. "Can you walk?"

I looked down at my feet as if they would give me an answer and he cursed at himself.

"That was a stupid question. I'm going to pick you up and carry you out of here, okay? The movement might hurt," he said apologetically.

I gave the smallest nod, and he leaned down to place his

arms under my knees.

"Finn," I stopped him with a hand on his chest. "I—my pants."

He looked down at me and realization settled in his features. "It's okay, come on now. Let me get you out of here before Art comes and murders me himself."

This time I let him lift me and tried to muffle my groans from the pain that shot through my whole body at the movement. He carried me toward the door, and I finally remembered Cain. Panic flooded my system, and I expected to hear a gunshot at any moment as he came in to find Finn carrying me out like a white knight.

I didn't realize I had said that aloud until Finn's hold on me tightened ever so slightly, "I appreciate the sentiment, but please don't mention that to Art, I value my life."

"You always make him sound so menacing," I said as we passed through the doorway. No one stood on the other side, and Finn took a left, heading in the opposite direction that I had when I tried to escape.

"That's because he is. Don't let the good looks and party boy persona fool you, you really don't want to get on his bad side."

Emotion suddenly clogged my throat. I wanted desperately to get to know this bad side of him, I wanted to live, to publish another article, to watch Vi dance in a ballet.

Finn mistook my emotions for pain and he apologized again, "We're almost there, I promise."

"Vi," I managed to croak out.

"She's at the hotel, only because I absolutely refused to let her come with me. She'll meet you as soon as you're out of here."

She was at the hotel? She had talked to Finn? How? I had no idea, but I wasn't the least bit surprised. Fresh tears rolled down my cheeks as I thought of her.

"Shh," he quietly soothed as we made it into the elevator and down to the ground level. As we exited, I could now see that the building we were in appeared to be an old, vacant office building. We made it outside, and the feeling of the sweet air on my face sent another wave of tears. I was shocked that I hadn't run out of them by now.

Finn stopped at the passenger seat and settled me in before running to the driver's side. He had just slid in when his phone rang. He started the car and gunned it away from the building before answering. "I got her."

"Ava," the sound of his deep voice sent a sob ripping through me. I didn't think I'd ever hear it again.

"Baby girl," he murmured through the phone, and I pulled myself together enough to respond.

"Hey."

"Hey, pretty lady."

A ridiculous laugh broke free, which turned into a groan.

"Stop that," Finn scolded him. "Where are you?"

There was a moment of silence on the other end of the line, and I wondered if the call had dropped. Art finally spoke. "Toni found him. Cain. I'm on my way there right now." There was something dark in his voice, and I resisted the urge to shiver as Finn's words played through my head.

"Art—" Finn started.

"Don't. Get her to the hospital, get Victoria, keep her safe. I'll be there as soon as I can."

"Be careful," I said, interrupting whatever Finn was going to say.

"Oh, little bird, don't worry about me. Worry about yourself, I'll be there as soon as I can," he repeated, and I nodded even though he couldn't see me. I finally leaned back against the seat rest and closed my eyes. Everything was going to be okay.

46

Art

I clenched the steering wheel until my knuckles turned white as I warred with myself over turning around and driving back to Ava.

Finn had her, he would protect her, but the image he'd sent me of her swollen and bruised in his front seat sent white hot anger through me, and I needed to be with her.

No, I needed to get to Cain.

I gritted my teeth and forced myself to keep following the directions from Toni. She'd found him at a small airfield, attempting to flee the country. He must have been alerted by someone that we were onto him, and he'd tucked his tail and fled. Would he have even given me Ava's location if I had wired him the money at midnight, or would he have simply left her to rot in the closet where Finn found her? His brief description of how he'd found her made my blood boil in my veins.

All of this because he felt entitled to my mom's company just because he was fucking her? I still didn't understand the other people he'd killed in the hotel, were they just random? He had plenty of money as COO, more than he should ever need, so what was this about, just power? Entitlement?

I turned off onto a dirt road and followed the winding curves until I pulled up at a small property with a long hangar and a landing strip. He was smart to avoid the big airports, knowing I could find him there. But he was an idiot to think I couldn't find him here. Toni was good. There was a reason people paid what they did for her services.

The gravel crunched beneath my shoes as I exited the car and approached the shed. There was no security footage here that Toni could access, but from what she'd found, there was a good chance Cain was here alone. Even still, I prepared to encounter innocent people here just in case. Although how innocent could they truly be if they associated with Cain?

I wished I could say I'd always known there was something off about him, but frankly, he was just like every other uptight prick I'd met over the years and, until Finn's list, I'd never suspected he was behind this.

I reached the door and opened it with a hard tug. I was guessing Cain hadn't intended on barricading himself in here, instead he was focused on getting out while he could. Toni didn't think he had left yet, but on the off chance she was wrong, I would need to come up with a plan B, because, unfortunately, piloting was not in my repertoire.

Luck was on my side, as I heard movement and swearing down the length of the hangar, and I could taste vengeance on my tongue, the anticipation of it so sweet. Reaching the small plane, I found him inside the cockpit already, and without a second thought, I lifted my arm and shot a hole in the side of the aircraft.

"What the fuck?" he shouted as he turned to look out the window and saw me with my gun pointed in the direction of his head, smiling, all teeth.

"Hello, Cain."

He made to reach for something that I could only assume was a gun, but before he had a chance to, I pulled the trigger and sent a bullet through his window. He screamed as the glass shattered around him, and I tsked as I stepped closer.

"I'd appreciate if you'd stop moving. I'd really hate to cut this short sooner than intended."

I reached through the broken window and with a quick move opened the door and pulled him to the concrete floor. He howled in pain as he fell on glass, and I kept my gun trained on him as I performed a quick pat-down, finding his gun in his waistband. I admired it appreciatively, and he finally looked up to glare at me through his pain.

"What are you doing here?"

"Oh, Cain, we are way past that." When he didn't bother to reply, I continued. "What was your plan here? What did you really think would happen in all of this? You'd get a mil and suddenly life would be what you wanted it to be?"

"You don't deserve the hotel, you didn't do jack shit, I spent years making it what it has become," he snarled.

"That may be true, but do you really think that your dick is so impressive you were somehow going to fuck Laurie into giving it to you?"

"She was going to before she died," he spat.

"Actually, I'm pretty sure she was just saying that to get you into bed with her, but regardless," I waved his own gun at him when he started to continue, "She's gone, it's in my name, and you really thought going after my girl would be the way to get what you want?"

"She's dead, I killed her before I left," he lied through bared teeth.

"Okay, first off, you're a terrible liar, and secondly, you drastically underestimate me. And the people I know. Lucky for you, she was found alive, which means there's s good chance you make it out of here alive as well."

Cain's face blanched as he finally began to understand the situation he was in.

"Now get up."

He did as I commanded, and I waved my gun toward the direction I had come.

"I'm pretty sure I passed an office on my way in here, if you would be so kind as to lead the way."

He did, and we found ourselves in a small office filled with loose papers. I yanked a metal chair from behind the desk to the middle of the room and motioned with my gun for him to sit. When he refused, I pointed my gun at his left shoulder and pulled the trigger.

A scream tore through him, and I used the opportunity to push him into the chair. He clutched his injured shoulder, and I made quick work of securing him to the chair with an extension cord I found lying on the desk.

I stepped back to survey my work. "Now, that's much better."

"You're going to kill me over a bitch?!" he screeched at me.

"No, I'm going to torture you because of a beautiful woman who happens to be mine."

He continued to glare at me, and I pulled up a picture on my phone.

"Thankfully, a friend of mine was kind enough to send me a picture of her after he got her out of that abandoned warehouse. Kinda like this, huh?" I said, waving my gun around the room.

Anger and pain tore through me as I took in her injuries on the screen, from her swollen black eye to her bloody, matted hair and the broken nails on her right hand. How had she broken her nails? Had she tried to fight him off?

As soon as the thought popped into my head, I almost ended it right then and there with a bullet to his head, but after some practiced deep breathing, I regained a semblance of control.

"I'll be back," I said as left the room. I knew he wasn't expecting me to leave him now, and I could imagine the confusion that would turn into the one thing that would hurt the most—hope.

I found what I was looking for rather quickly, a toolbox filled with all sorts of equipment. I carried it back to the office, where I found Cain frantically twisting in his chair, attempting to free himself.

"Almost," I said as I entered, and he swung back to look at me with wide eyes.

"I have to be honest with you, I have a dilemma."

He didn't answer, but I didn't expect him to. I continued on as I set the toolbox on the desk. "You see, I really want to go see Ava for myself, but I also can't let you go unpunished. An eye for an eye as they say, right?"

I picked up a pair of pliers and tested them out. These should work. "I've always had a thing for symmetry, my mom wasn't like that, so I blame my mystery sperm donor. Anyway, I'm getting off track. My point is," I said as I stopped at his right side. "This is going to hurt."

I reached down with the pliers and ripped off the nail on his pointer finger. He screamed so loud my ears began to ring, and I resisted the urge to cover them. I was sure I could find a pair of sound cancelling headphones in here somewhere, but I was already getting antsy to leave.

I reached for his hand again, and he did his best to fight me, but it was no use. I clamped the pliers onto the nail of his middle finger and pulled that one off with a *pop*.

His screams grew louder, which was actually kind of impressive. I stepped back to admire my work and then nodded as he continued to whimper. Suddenly, I was in his face, growling out, "How did she get her black eye?"

"She-she fell down the stairs," he stuttered.

"Ahh," I said as I stepped back just as quickly as I had approached. "Unfortunately, we don't have any stairs here."

And then I gripped his bloody shoulder and punched him directly in the face. He screamed in pain, and I bit my tongue to distract from the burning in my own fist as I shook it out.

"You fucking piece of shit!" he screeched as he spat blood at me. I turned my back on him to place the tools back in the box. Just like that, my fury had subsided, and now I was left hollow, with a desperate need to see, smell, touch Ava.

"You're worthless, your own mom didn't even want you, you are going to lose the hotel, and someone else is going to end up fucking your girl like a whore."

I went completely still, my hand still on the toolbox. Slowly, I turned to him, and all I saw was rage and satisfaction in his rapidly swelling face as he glared back at me.

"You know how earlier I said I wasn't going to kill you?" Silence. "I lied." Then I shot him in the face and walked out of the hanger.

47

Ava

I was getting really sick of waking to a pounding headache. I groaned before even opening my eyes and heard shuffling feet and the most beautiful sound in the world.

"Nurse! She's waking up!"

I groaned again as I attempted to shift my weight and relieve the ache in my side.

"Hey, hey, don't move," came Vi's voice again. Finally, and with great effort, I pried my eyes open to see her concerned gaze peering back at me.

"Hey," I croaked.

"Hey back," she said with a smile that didn't quite meet her eyes. "How are you feeling?"

"Like hell," I responded.

"Well, you look as beautiful as ever," came a familiar voice beside me, and I turned to see Finn lounging in a chair against the far wall.

"Has anyone ever told you you're a terrible liar?" I rasped.

"Just about everyone," he said with a grin.

A nurse came through the doors and stopped at the side of the bed, handing me a cup of ice chips. "I'm Lili, your nurse for the evening. How are you feeling?" she asked in a beautiful Filipino accent.

I swallowed a few of the chips before answering. "I've been better."

She laughed, and the sound was light and warm. "I would imagine so given your bruised ribs and concussion."

"So, I didn't break anything?"

"No, you did not," she said as she began typing on her computer.

"So, when can I go home then?"

She laughed again. "Considering you just woke up from your concussed nap, I'm pretty sure the doctor is planning on holding off on discharge until the morning."

I'm sure she could see my disappointment with that answer, and she nodded to the clock. "Visiting hours are almost over, and then I would suggest taking full advantage of the pain medication, and before you know it, it will be morning, and you can break out of here."

I nodded, resigned, and adjusted myself in the bed. That small movement caused a sharp pain in my side that I did my best to conceal, but my nurse could see it anyway and she gave me a knowing smile.

"Would you like me to get you something now?"

"Yes please," I murmured.

"Here's your call light if you need anything. I'll be right back."

She left and I turned to Vi and Finn. 'There's so much I want to know." Finn had brought me straight here and I'd passed out before Vi showed up or I'd really been able to get any information out of him.

"We can catch you up later," Vi said as she sat on the edge of my bed and grabbed my hand.

"Are you okay if I crash at your place when I leave here?"

"Umm, I would be offended if you didn't," she said sternly.

That settled, I turned to Finn. "Where's Art?"

A pained look passed over his face before he cleared his throat. "He went to try to catch up with Cain before he fled the country. He'll be over as soon as he can."

"Visiting hours are almost up she said, which is probably for the best, cause my head is starting to kill me again."

"Concussions are not for the weak. I once got knocked in the head so hard that I couldn't see straight for like a week," Finn piped up from his spot.

"I'm afraid to ask how that happened," I said with a chuckle that sent pain through my side.

"Oh, it was in a boxing match. But don't worry, I've improved since then," he said with a wink.

"Did you drive here?" I asked, turning my attention back to Vi.

"No, Finn picked me up."

"I can drop her off," Finn said, and was that excitement I heard in his voice?

"Do you have a way to call me?" Vi asked, scanning my room. I motioned to the hospital phone on the table.

"Yeah, I'm sure I can figure out how to use that."

"Call me when you have a discharge time, and I'll come by to pick you up tomorrow," Vi said, giving my hand a squeeze. I felt tears prick my eyes as I squeezed back.

"Thanks, Vi," I said in a husky voice.

Thankfully, Lili chose that moment to reenter, and the other two picked up their belongings to head out.

"Enjoy the drugs," Vi said with a wink. "I'll get your space all set up for you."

They left, and Lili made quick work of my medication before leaving me alone. The silence felt heavy, but before panic could take hold, my eyelids grew heavy, and I fell asleep.

48

Art

I was in shock. I hadn't gone in there intending to kill him. I was angry and I wanted to make him pay, but I had just ended a life. And now there was a dead body in that hanger. I did the only thing I could think of.

"Toni," she answered on the first ring.

"He's dead." I said in way of greeting. Silence.

"At the address I sent you?"

"Yes."

"I'll handle it."

"I didn't mean to—"

"I'll handle it," she said again, cutting me off. I nodded even though she couldn't see me.

"I found something else."

My knuckles tensed on the wheel as I waited for her to go on.

"Does the name Kim Parly mean anything to you?"

I tried to think back. "Yeah, I think she was the one who came with Ava to interview me a couple times."

"Yeah, it looks like she's the senior publisher at the *Manhattan Press.* I found some odd correspondences between her and Cain."

"Odd how?"

"He was specifically asking her to come out to interview you, he passed on some details of the murders at your hotel and just looked like he was feeding her information."

"Did she know about the abduction?" I waited for her response, and the next few moments would determine Kim's fate.

"Not from anything I can find. It looks more like she was just using Cain for the publicity and articles."

I let out the breath I'd been holding. So, she was just a bitch and not complicit in kidnapping and murder. "Thanks for the info. Can you get me an address for her?"

"Already sent over."

"I owe you."

"Don't worry, I fully plan on having you make it up to me."

I didn't know what her request would be, money or some future favor, but after what she'd done in helping save Ava, there wasn't much I wouldn't give her.

I ended the call just to see another call coming through. Finn.

Panic surged through me as I answered Finn's call, "What?"

"Nice to hear from you too, man."

"What is it," I ground out.

"Jeez, man, I was just calling to tell you that Vi and I just left because visiting hours are over, and Ava was gonna crash for the night."

"And?"

"And I thought maybe you'd like to know that before you drive all the way there?"

I laughed, but it held no humor. Visiting hours were not about to stop me.

"Also, if I can give you a word of advice," he continued.

I growled but he ignored me.

"Fix your fecking attitude. Ava has just been through a traumatic ordeal, and regardless of your feelings on the matter, she doesn't need you stomping about."

I wanted to respond that he didn't know what was best for her, but I stopped when I let a little bit of common sense leak in. I was being an ass, even I could admit that. So instead, I grudgingly responded, "Fine."

He laughed, "See? Told you I was a miracle worker."

"Who are you talking to?"

"I'm giving Vi a ride home."

"Vi?" I questioned as my eyebrows shot up.

"Sorry, you're breaking up, gotta go, talk to you later." And then the asshat hung up on me.

I sighed and pulled up Kim's address. If Ava was going to sleep, I might as well get something useful done before heading over there.

I took the two hour drive to the address, thankful that the traffic was light this time of the evening, and arrived at a beautiful two-story home outside the city. There were several lights on inside the house. Hopefully she was home alone.

I knocked on the door, and it was opened by an older man.

"Can I help you?"

"Yeah, sorry for coming so late, but I'm needing to talk to Kim Parly."

"I don't think she's available right now."

I tried to keep my expression pleasant. "I understand. If you wouldn't mind telling her it's Arthur Michaels, I'm sure she would be interested in talking with me."

The man looked skeptical, but he nodded and said, "Let me go ask her," before closing the door, leaving me outside.

Smart man.

I heard footsteps and a moment later Kim opened the door.

"Arthur, this is a surprise."

"Hello, Kim, sorry for coming by so late, but I thought it might be worth it for you to get an in person exclusive."

Curiosity lit her gaze like I assumed it would. These piranhas were all the same.

"Sure, yeah, how about you come into my office."

I followed her into a comfortable office space, and she closed the door behind us before settling behind her desk. I took the seat across from her and leaned my elbows on my knees. "I'll get straight to the point."

"Direct, I like that."

"Ava was kidnapped yesterday by Cain Mathews, who then attempted to use her as a ransom." Genuine shock flashed through her eyes, and despite Toni's research, I was glad to see it.

"I—" she paused and seemed to contemplate her next words. "Why are you telling me this?"

"I know that you were talking to Cain quite a bit over the last several weeks." Her mouth opened and then closed again without a word.

"I also am aware that you fired Ava right before the kidnapping took place."

"If you are suggesting—"

"I'm not suggesting anything. However, if you want your correspondence with him to remain private, I think it would be best if Ava were offered a new position at the company. Something with a raise and promotion."

"Are you blackmailing me, Mr. Michaels?"

"Absolutely not, blackmail implies you did something wrong that I could use against you. I'm just letting you know from personal experience, if text messages are leaked without context, sometimes the public draws their own wrong conclusions." I stood, not giving her a chance to respond.

I was almost to the door when she asked, "Is Ava okay?"

"She will be," I answered. "Oh, one more thing," I said as I turned.

Kim met my gaze once again.

"I was drugged for that picture your company took of me at the club. Was that your doing?"

She swallowed but kept my gaze. "No. Cain told me there would be a good opportunity to catch you with some women at the club. That's all I knew."

She could be lying. And if she was, I would find out. But for now, I took her words at face value and exited her house.

By the time I made it back to the city, it was nearing midnight, and I contemplated going by the hospital, but the idea of disturbing Ava's much needed sleep filled me with too much guilt. Instead, I headed toward the hotel. I would catch a couple hours of sleep and then be over there before she discharged.

After the day I'd had, I was asleep before my head even hit the pillow.

49

Ava

I woke up the next morning feeling refreshed, which was something I never thought I'd say about being in the hospital. Even after being woken up every four hours, I had slept like a baby. Well, one of those babies who slept through the night, at least.

Lili ended her shift, and an older woman named Janet took over from there. When I shared my desire to get out of here as soon as I could, she said that she thought that would be possible. When the doctor came by for rounds, she said she had no problem with me discharging, and I immediately called Vi.

"Come pick me up please?"

"On my way! Coffee?"

"Oh my gosh, yes please." I could hear the smile in her voice when she hung up, promising to be there as soon as she ran through the drive through.

The only items in my hospital room were my dirty clothes from yesterday which Lili had been kind enough to put into a plastic bag for me. The thought of putting them back on sent my heart racing and I was relieved when my nurse gave me a pair of hospital scrubs to wear home instead.

As I dressed I thought over the last couple days. It seemed like a lifetime ago that I had come to the Laurie for my assignment, but it hadn't been that long. I guess that's what happened when you got kidnapped.

My thoughts turned to Art. Our relationship had been so up and down. A one night stand turned client-reporter turned more hookups and finally our dates. Things had seemed so nice, and then there was the article that had been published. I had almost forgotten about that in everything that followed. We still needed to talk about it. Or maybe we didn't, and whatever we had was over just in time for me to leave.

The thought caused my heart to ache, but truthfully, I had no idea what my future held. Career, relationship, anything. Regardless of what happened, though, I needed closure.

Thankfully, Vi arrived before I could let myself get too caught up in my feelings, and I gingerly walked to her car, which was mercifully close. She handed me my large, iced drink as I sat down, and I leaned over to kiss her cheek.

"You are the best person in the whole world," I told her, meaning every word.

She laughed and waved me off as we headed to her apartment. "I bet you say that to every person who brings you coffee and picks you up after you've been kidnapped by a psycho."

"Guilty," I said, taking another long drink of my coffee.

"You wanna talk about it?" she asked with a sideways glance in my direction.

"Let's just get home."

We rode the rest of the way in a comfortable silence, and she pulled up outside her building, then helped me inside, and, like promised, she had the living transformed into my sickbay. The couch was full of pillows and blankets, there were snacks on the table, and the TV was even set up with some trashy reality show.

I collapsed onto the couch and sighed heavily. I hadn't realized just how much walking would take it out of me.

"Do you need anything? Ibuprofen?"

"I took something before I left, I should be okay. And this looks perfect, thank you."

She beamed and settled down to share my makeshift bed. After several long moments of watching a show on mute, just settling in, she spoke up from beside me, "You know, you're more than welcome to stay here as long as you need, right?"

"I know. And as much as I'd love to stay here, I have to get home to pay my rent and everything."

"Move out of there! You said your lease is up soon anyway, and you haven't signed anything yet. Move in with me."

"Into your one bedroom apartment?"

"We can get something bigger! You know I've been wanting more space."

"And how am I supposed to help with rent? I was fired, you know. Actually, you probably don't know. So, yeah, I was fired."

"I did know," Vi said, almost sheepishly. "When I went to Art's place and found out he hadn't talked to you in a while, I called your boss and was told you didn't work there any longer."

"You talked to Kim?" I asked incredulously.

"Well, actually, I think it was just somebody who answers phones. What happened, anyway?"

"I refused to continue writing the piece on Art. I told her I wanted to do something else, and she said I could go."

"What a bitch."

I nodded in agreement.

"Anyway," she continued. "My point was that you'll get

another job. You're smart and motivated, and anybody would be lucky to have you. Just get out of your lease and move in with me."

That sounded amazing, and I snuggled in closer to her.

"I'll think about it."

It was a lie and we both knew it. Without a steady income, there was no way I would do that, but I could live in this fantasy a little longer.

As if on cue, my phone rang. I thought about ignoring it but finally picked it up and was shocked to see Kim's name on the screen.

"Hello?"

"Is this Ava?"

"Yeah, this is Ava." A pause.

"Ava, this is Kim." Another pause. "I heard about your incident, and wanted to see how you were doing."

My *incident*? And from who?

"I'm okay," I said hesitantly. "I was discharged this morning, nothing too serious."

"That's good, that's good."

I had nothing to say to her, so I let the silence linger until she spoke again.

"I'm sure my call comes as a bit of a surprise," she said, and if I didn't know better, I would say I heard sarcasm in her voice.

"Yeah, I definitely wasn't expecting to hear from you."

"Well, I was just calling because there has been a sudden vacancy in a position here, and I wanted to see if you'd be interested."

Vi must have seen my shock, because she nudged me and mouthed *what*? I shook my head and focused back on the conversation. "Oh, um."

"It's a senior position in the same department you've been in. There's a pay increase and—" she continued talking, but I didn't hear any of it. She was offering me a job? With a raise and promotion?

I couldn't wrap my mind around what was happening. Just because she'd heard I got kidnapped? Was this a pity offer? But that didn't make any sense. Kim would never do anything out of pity, let alone offer me a job.

I realized she had stopped talking, and I cleared my throat. "Yeah, I would definitely be interested in that. I'm still recovering, and I don't know when I'll be cleared to go back to work—"

"Yes, of course. We can work out the details later. In the meantime, good luck with your recovery. Let me know if there's anything we can do for you." With that, she ended the call.

"What. The. Fuck?" I exclaimed.

"What on earth was that about?" Vi asked, having watched my reaction the entire conversation.

"Kim just offered me my job back. Well, kind of, she offered me a promotion and raise along with it."

Vi's face mirrored how I felt. "Maybe she just needed some time to realize what a bitch she was."

"I'm so confused right now," I said..

"Well, honestly I don't care what caused her change of heart, you wanna know why?"

"Why?"

"Because now you have no reason not to move in with me!"

I laughed but realized she was right. I'd spent too long dragging my feet, staying in situations I didn't like. It was time to do something for myself.

"Fine, let's do some apartment hunting."

My sentence was cut off by her squeal as she lunged for her laptop, and I laughed as I settled in to watch her. Maybe everything would be okay after all.

50

Art

I woke up to a loud buzzing noise and looked over to see my phone lighting up on my nightstand. Finn.

"Yes," I answered groggily.

"I just wanted to see how Ava's doing." Ava. Oh my god.

"What time is it?" I asked, pulling away my phone to glance at the time. 11:03. Shit.

"Fuck, I overslept."

"Oh damn, sorry for waking you up, I just assumed you'd already be there."

"Yeah, I was planning on it but I must have gone to another dimension while I slept, because I definitely don't remember turning my alarm off this morning."

"You needed it. I'm sure she's fine, Vi was planning on picking her up this morning after discharge, I'm sure she's fine." He said again.

I was still angry at myself for oversleeping but happy that Vi had gone to pick her up. "Any chance you have her address?" I asked as I hurriedly dressed. He passed it along and I hung up before waving off breakfast and making my way downstairs.

It was a short drive over to her apartment complex, where I knocked and waited impatiently as I heard footsteps approach the door. Vi opened it with, "Took you long enough."

I glared at her and motioned inside. "Can I come in?"

"Are you gonna be an ass to her again?" I opened my mouth to protest but closed it again before shaking my head. Whatever she'd been told from Ava was justified, and while Ava may have forgiven me, that didn't mean Vi had.

"Fine," she said, letting me in. Ava was sitting on the couch, cuddled under a mountain of blankets, watching something on TV. She looked up as I approached, and a hesitant smile stretched across her face. "Hey."

"Hey back."

"I'll be in my room," Vi said with a pointed look at me before grabbing her laptop and leaving us alone.

"How are you feeling?" I asked as I approached and slid onto the couch.

"I've been better, but I don't feel as bad as I look," she said with a small laugh. Tension hung in the air, and I hated it.

Even when we'd been actively arguing and avoiding each other, it didn't feel like this awkward thing between us.

"About the article."

"I tried to call you."

We spoke at the same time, and I forged on when she stopped. "I was drugged."

"What?!"

"That night I went out with Finn and his buddies. I only had like one drink, and I blacked out and can't remember most of the night. I woke up so sick, and Finn thinks they slipped me something to get the pictures and article."

She didn't say anything, and I leaned closer to grab her

hands. "Ava, I swear to you, I did not agree to have some chick on my lap, I would never do that shit to you."

"I was so mad. And embarrassed," a tear slipped free, and it broke my heart. I pulled her into me and rubbed her shoulder as she quietly cried.

"You have every right to be mad, it looked awful."

"I kept telling myself maybe there was more to the story, but I couldn't figure out how."

"I'm so sorry, baby, I didn't mean to do that to you."

She pulled back angrily. "Don't apologize. You're the one who was drugged!"

I gently tugged her back into my side. "Hey, I'm fine. It's you I'm worried about."

"He told me you wanted to meet for lunch."

It took me a second to follow the change of topic. Cain. Anger surged through me, and I almost wished he was alive so I could shoot him again.

"I called a ride, and somehow the person who showed up was in on it too, and she brought me to this underground garage where... *he* was waiting, and he had a gun. I was so confused and scared, I didn't know what he wanted."

"He was trying to use you to get to me," I said as shame crawled through me.

"But what did he want?"

"Money, power, the company. He was having an affair with my mom and felt entitled to my share of the business. I got a text from an unknown number that a friend of mine traced back to him. After that, we were able to find where he stashed you, I just wish I had known he had taken you sooner."

"I left you a message before I left the hotel, and I was going to go to Vi's house, but then..." her voice trailed off.

"Vi came to my place to find you, you know. She's the reason we figured out something had happened. She's a good friend."

"The best," she said as she snuggled in deeper to my side.

I would be content to sit in this exact spot all day, but then her stomach growled, and she covered it sheepishly. "Sorry."

"Now who's apologizing for something they have no business apologizing for? Do you want me to order some food?"

"Could we go somewhere instead?"

When I looked at her in surprise, she laughed and waved a hand at herself. "Maybe like a drive through or something so I don't scare anyone. I just want some fresh air."

"Absolutely. Do you need to bring anything?"

"No, just let me tell Vi."

I helped her off the couch, and she popped her head into the bedroom before meeting me at the door. I held out my hand and she slipped hers into it. There had been awhile there where I wondered if I'd ever get to feel her skin against mine again. The thought sent a fresh wave of anger through me, and it must have been obvious because Ava squeezed my hand.

"I'm okay," she whispered.

I brought her hand up to my mouth and pressed a kiss to it before leading her down to my car.

As requested, we went through a drive through and got two large, greasy burgers with a bucket of fries and a couple milkshakes. Then I parked overlooking a lake so we could feel the wind through the open windows as we ate our lunch.

"Vi wants me to move in with her," she said, breaking the silence.

"I like that plan." She laughed, and I shrugged.

"It's easier than me having to find a house closer to your apartment."

Her mouth dropped open in the cutest expression. "You wouldn't."

"Is that a challenge?" I asked with a smirk. She smacked

my arm and went back to her burger.

"I told her no because I'm currently unemployed, but then Kim, my old boss, called me."

"Did she?" I said nonchalantly.

"Yeah, she said she'd heard about my 'incident' and wanted to check on me and offer me a new position."

"Well, that's nice. You deserve it."

"You didn't happen to have anything to do with her recent change of heart, did you?"

"My dear, you flatter me," I said, pressing a hand to my chest in mock humility. "The fact that you assume that I have such sway."

"So you didn't have anything to do with it?" she pressed, and the smile dropped from my face.

"I might have talked to her and shared that it would be in her best interest to reinstate your employment."

"You threatened her?"

"No," I said honestly. "Well, maybe you'd call it that, but I told her that I'd found some correspondence between her and Cain and that they might get leaked. If she'd done nothing wrong, she wouldn't have been worried about them getting out. Okay, so maybe I threatened her, but I was only threatening to tell the truth."

Ava stared at me for a long moment before popping another fry in her mouth. "I see. I don't know if I'm going to take it. I don't know if I want to work for someone who only agreed to hire me back for fear of getting in trouble."

"That's your decision. I think you should, I think you deserve something for all the shit she gave you over me and that article. But if you aren't comfortable with that, then I have no doubt you will get a great position at another company."

"Why, cause you'll call them and tell them they have to hire me?"

"You don't need me to do that, you're more than capable of landing a job on your own." Pause. "But yes, I have no problems calling in a favor if they don't see your potential."

"Is this what it's like dating you?"

"Oh, this and so much more." I said, leaning in to steal a fry from her.

"Hmmm," she hummed in response.

"You think you're up to the task?"

"I guess there's only one way to find out," she said, and the heat in her gaze was like a shot straight to my groin. I attempted to readjust myself and she watched the movement with a smirk. "You gonna take us somewhere a little more private?"

"What about the no sex just communication rule you set?" I asked, trying my best to get my cock to calm down.

"I think I've had enough talking for now," she said, the hunger in her eyes doing insane things to me.

"Baby, you just got out of the hospital, I don't want to hurt you even more."

"It's just bruises, I'm fine. You need to hear an all clear from my doctor?" she said pulling out her phone.

"Even still, they look painful," I argued.

"Honestly, I think it's a fitting representation of us. A little bruised around the edges."

When I didn't immediately respond, she sat back in her seat.

"Fine. I've never begged for attention, and I'm not about to start now. If you don't want to fuck me, I'm sure I can find someone who will."

Before I even knew what I was doing, I'd reached across and ripped the phone out of her hand. I was tempted to throw it out the window but instead dropped it into my lap.

"Like hell you will." The smirk on her face told me she knew she'd won. I ground my molars but admitted defeat as I backed out of the parking space and drove us onto the highway. She didn't ask where we were going, and I didn't volunteer the information as I drove, one hand holding her thigh. Either it was my imagination, or she kept scooting herself down in her chair, forcing my hand higher and higher. I was about to say fuck it and pull her onto my lap right then and there, when I finally pulled up to a tall building.

"Where are we?" she finally asked.

"My hotel."

"This isn't the Laurie."

"I just bought it right before all of this went down. We haven't made an official switch yet, only a handful of people know. But I thought it would be a better place than the Laurie right now."

The gratitude in her eyes told me I had made the right decision. We walked inside and I checked us into the nicest room they had. The receptionist didn't recognize me, and it was strangely nice feeling like a normal couple. We made it up to the suite, and Ava gasped as we stepped inside. "This is beautiful."

It really was. There was a Jacuzzi tub in the middle of the foyer, with a waterfall pouring into it. There was a full kitchenette and a California king with silk sheets. But despite the luxury around us, I couldn't take my eyes off her.

"I would love to go swimming, but I didn't pack a suit," she said, turning to face me.

"Perfect," I responded as my eyes roamed her body.

"Oh?" She said, stepping backward towards the pool and slowly pulling off her oversized t-shirt. I nearly groaned at the sight of her in a black bra that displayed her cleavage beautifully. Next, she stepped out of her shorts, and I did groan then, staring at her gorgeous body, dressed only in her underwear. I stalked toward her, and she pulled off her bra, letting her breasts bounce free, maintaining eye contact the whole time. I wanted to reach out and touch them, but she turned her back to me and bent down to step out of her underwear, giving me a full view of her plump ass.

"Ava," I groaned, and she stood up again and turned back toward me.

"You gonna join me?" she said before stepping into the water.

Fuck me. I tore my clothes off much quicker than she had, and she laughed as I joined her in the hot water.

"You know how many people have had sex in here?" I asked as I closed in on her.

"You really know how to set the mood, don't you?" she asked as she propped her elbows on the edge of the pool, letting her breasts rest gloriously above the water.

I prowled closer and placed my hands on either side of her on the pool edge before leaning down to suck one of her nipples into my mouth. She gasped as she arched her back, pressing her breast further into me. I pulled back and began pressing kisses to her chest while moving to the other nipple.

"You. Scared. The. Shit. Out. Of. Me." I said between kisses before sucking the other nipple into my mouth and massaging her other breast with my hand.

Her moan grew in pitch as I pinched the nipple between my fingers, and I pulled back and stared deep into her eyes. "I thought I was going to die from fear when I realized you had been taken."

"I'm right here," she said, bringing her hands up to frame my face. She had one hell of a nasty black eye, and scrapes and bruises marred her face, chest, and arms. Yet nothing had ever looked more perfect, more angelic, more mine.

"Never again," I swore, and she nodded before pulling my face into hers for a bruising kiss. I tried to be gentle, not wanting to cause her pain, but her tongue ravaged my mouth like she was consuming me. I reached down into the water and lifted her by her perfect ass to set her on the edge of the pool without breaking the kiss. At this angle, she had to lean down to kiss me, and her wet hair fell into our faces, cool against the heat we were producing. I pulled back and began a slow path of kisses on her chest again, down her stomach and toward her pelvis. She tried to buck against me, but I kept my hands gripped tight on her hips.

"Art," she groaned.

"Shhh, let me taste you. I've missed this body so fucking much. You're perfection, baby, I could survive solely on the taste of you."

She obliged and leaned back against her hands while she watched me work with heavy lids. I moved my hands to her knees and spread her legs, almost stopping when I saw the bruises on her thighs, but I reminded myself that the man responsible was dead. I continued my slow exploration, gently kissing each bruise in a featherlight touch. Her responding gasps spurred me on, and I pulled her ass to the edge of the pool as I spread her legs far enough to expose her perfect pussy.

"Every time I think I've decided what my favorite part of you is, I change my mind when I remember the others. But this, goddamn, this is one of my favorites," I said before burying my face between her legs. She tasted like salt and the flavor that was uniquely her. So fucking sweet on my tongue. She bucked against me, and this time I let her as she pulled my face deeper into her vagina. I swirled my tongue on her clit until I found the rhythm that she liked, and she began to beg.

"Yes, please, oh my god, Art." I kept the same pace, and in a moment, she broke apart, coming all over my face.

When her writhing had subsided, I stood up and pressed my lips to hers.

"I need you inside me," she said as she clung to me. That

was all she needed to say, and I was out of the pool, following her to the king bed. I went to push her onto the comforter when she shook her head. "Lay down."

"Yes, ma'am," I said with a smirk, curious where this was going. I laid on my back, thoroughly enjoying the sight of her climbing onto the mattress and crawling up me. She stared at me with heavy lids before grabbing my cock and slipping it into her mouth without breaking eye contact.

"Oh my god, Ava."

"Hmm," she hummed against me, and the sound was electricity to my veins. She pulled back all the way, and I heard the pop as I sprung free of her mouth, her fingers stroking down my shaft before cupping my balls and sliding me back into her wet mouth again. If it was possible to die of sensation overload, that was about to happen to me. The warmth of her mouth, the pressure of her hand, I was going to implode.

She took me so deep that I touched the back of her throat and she gagged against me. My hips involuntarily lifted from the bed as I pumped into her.

"Ava, please," it was my turn to beg.

She looked up at me and understood the desire on my face as she released my cock to crawl up me and straddle my hips. She reached down to guide me inside her, and I groaned at the sensation of sliding into her wet heat.

"You are perfection, you are everything I could ever want in this world," I said as she began to ride me. And I meant every word of it. Seeing her like this, naked and in control on top of me, I would do anything for her. Give up my business, all of my money, burn the world if she just asked.

She rode me with every ounce of energy and passion that she had, and all too soon, I was coming inside her, moaning her name. Once we had both come down from our highs, I rolled us so that we faced each other on our sides, still a tangle of limbs and sweat.

"I think I'll keep you, Arthur Samual Michaels," she said as she traced my face with her fingertip.

Of course in all her research of me she'd found my middle name. I couldn't even be irritated though, I liked my name on her tongue way too much. "Like you have a choice." I said instead.

She cocked a brow, and I laughed. "Honey, you were mine from the moment you let me have the barstool next to you."

She scoffed and swatted at me. "Of course you'd like to think so."

I smirked and gave her a knowing look as I leaned in and kissed her slowly, savoring her taste. I'd let her think otherwise, but I'd always know the truth. She was made for me. Mine. Always mine.

51

Ava

It had been a week since my kidnapping, and I was back at the Laurie in the same conference room as that first meeting. This time, however, I was here as Art's girlfriend and support rather than a journalist.

Kim was here too, along with another junior journalist, who was my replacement. I had chosen to take her up on the job offer, with Art and Vi's encouragement, but I was also open to the idea of moving to a different company if the chance arose. I was still on leave, recovering, so this was the first time I had actually seen her in person. There was an uncomfortable feeling in the air, but I was so focused on Art that thoughts of her fell away easily. We were here to officially replace Cain's position as chief operating officer.

The day I was released, the New York police department had put out another press release announcing Cain as the murderer and also kidnapper, although they had thankfully kept my name out of it. I had every belief that that was because of Art.

The press release had stated that Cain had been found dead in a plane accident as he was attempting to flee the country. Based on conversations I had overheard between Art and Finn, I didn't entirely believe that his death was an accident. I was too afraid of the truth, however, so I opted not to ask Art about it. For once, I let my curiosity take a back seat.

I was pulled from my thoughts by Art squeezing my hand, and I looked up at him with a smile, still in awe that this man was mine. He cleared his throat, and the chattering around the room subsided.

"Thank you all for coming today. I thought it was best to have an official handing off of the position of COO. I know that these last several weeks have been some of the most eventful in the Laurie's history, but I wholeheartedly believe that this next change will have a positive impact on the company."

He waved toward the woman sitting on the other side of him, and she gave a warm smile. "Tanya Lopez has been with the company for years, and since taking on the position of general manager here at the New York branch, we have seen some amazing changes. I am very pleased to welcome her as the new COO of Laurie hotels."

There was some applause, and as she stood to speak, I couldn't help but continue to stare at Art. His first few weeks of CEO had been pure baptism by fire. What other person took over a company and the same day got thrust into a murder investigation? And while we had not exactly started off on the right foot, I couldn't help admire him now. The way he commanded a room, how he took any problem he was faced with head on, how he appeared fearless even when he was quaking inside.

"Careful, little bird," he whispered, leaning in close. "You keep looking at me like that, and I'm going to have to clear this room immediately."

I shivered at the feel of his warm breath on my ear, and the implication. "You wouldn't," I murmured back.

"Don't tempt me," he responded.

The thing was, I actually did believe him. And while he might have all of the authority to do that, I would die of embarrassment from being the cause of the disruption. So instead, I moved my gaze from his and looked back at the room of people gathered here. My eyes landed on Kim, and I thought of the recent news reports.

One of the articles that had been published this week was in regard to the arrest of the woman who had helped Cain kidnap me. Her name was Sarah, and she had been found in her basement with a gunshot wound to her foot. She had plead guilty to her involvement but had taken a plea deal in exchange for information regarding Cain and all that he had done.

With her help, they had discovered that Cain was the one who had snuck into the security room to tamper with the videos. The security guard on duty had been fired, but no one else had been found complicit. Art was convinced that there were people on the police force who had been working with Cain, but so far he had not been able to prove it. Finn was passionate about doing his own investigation into that.

The final person who had been arrested in this whole mess was the cocktail waitress at the club who had drugged Art. She admitted that Cain had asked her to slip something into his drink in exchange for a large sum of money. I had been maybe a little too excited to see reports of her arrest.

"Ready to get out of here?" Art asked, dipping his head close to me. I blinked and looked around the room at the people shuffling out.

"Is it over?"

He laughed as he tucked a strand of hair behind my ear,

one of his favorite habits, I had learned. "Yep, meetings been over for a while, while you've been daydreaming about me."

"I have not," I argued.

He smirked. "Wanna bet?"

"What if I said yes?"

"I would say that would make you a very smart woman indeed," he said, lifting me in one smooth motion and placing me on the conference table facing him.

"Art," I squeaked, thankful that the last person had already left the room.

"Mhm," he murmured into my neck as he pulled my body flush against his.

"What are you doing," I breathed, as he pressed his hips into mine, his erection proof that he had been doing some daydreaming of his own.

"I'm planning on fucking *my* woman on *my* table in *my* hotel."

"You are not," I gasped as he nipped my ear and slid his hand around to cup my breast.

"I beg to differ," he said as he reached up and tweaked my nipple through my shirt. My head fell back as white hot pleasure shot straight through me, and it took everything in me to contain my moan.

"What if someone hears us?"

"Then I will simply fire them so they never have the opportunity to hear a sound from you again," he said, pinching the other nipple.

"Art," I moaned, unable to help myself, and the sound unleashed him. He reached down and pulled my shirt off, exposing my hard nipples that were begging to be released from my bralette. He obliged, and I was left topless, sitting on the table. I didn't doubt that he would follow through with his promise to fire anyone who heard us, but also the thought of someone accidentally walking in on us made my thighs clench. Maybe I did have a little bit of an exhibitionist in me.

He leaned down, sucking one of my nipples into his mouth while he used his hand to play with the other.

"Oh, God, please," I begged as my core began to throb.

"Were you imagining this when you couldn't stop thinking about me during the meeting?" he murmured before moving his mouth to the other nipple.

"Oh God, yes, yes," I chanted, arching my back to give him better access. He chuckled against me, and I squirmed, attempting to rub my clit against him.

He pulled back and stared at me hungrily. "What do you want, Ava?"

I knew how much he liked to hear exactly what I wanted him to do to me. He had a little sub in him. And while it was a little out of my comfort zone to verbalize exactly what I wanted, I was finding that I loved it too.

"I want you to strip these pants off me, kiss my pussy through my underwear, and when I can't take it anymore, I want you to tear my thong off and eat me out until I come all over your face."

He groaned and fisted himself through his pants. I loved the power I had over him. My big, strong, billionaire CEO turned into an absolute puddle at my feet.

I barely had time to take a breath before he was doing exactly as I told him. My pants went flying across the room, and then he was pressing kisses all over my thighs and pussy. Soft and teasing and then a little harder, then barely there. I was going to lose my mind. I was going to burst into a million flames, and there would be nothing left of me. The pleasure pulsing through me, it was all too much and not enough.

"Art," I begged, but he didn't stop. I had asked for this, and he knew how much I loved the foreplay. And I did, but I didn't know how much more I could take of this.

"Baby, please," I begged again, almost sobbing at the need to feel him against my skin. He pressed one more soft kiss to my clit through my underwear before tearing them off me in pieces, exactly as I had requested.

I felt the rush of cool air against my burning skin before he leaned back in and gave me the slowest lick from ass to clit. I couldn't take another second of this. I reached forward and grabbed his head, forcing him into me. He groaned against me, and for the briefest moment I hoped I wasn't suffocating him before I pushed the thought aside and fucked his face like I would die if I didn't.

He gave me everything, lavishing my body in the way that only he could, and before long, my body finally reached its peak and I tumbled over, moaning his name as I rocked my vagina against him until I was spent. He pulled back, and I noticed how he was still fully clothed while I sat naked.

"That's not fair," I said, pointing to his suit.

"Come upstairs with me, and we can rectify that situation." He said, handing me my shirt.

"Don't mind if I do," I responded pulling it over my head. He went to step away to get my pants, but I pulled him back to me and kissed him deeply.

"What was that for?" he asked, keeping his forehead pressed to mine.

"I'm just so grateful. For this. You. Us."

He leaned closer and brushed the softest kiss against my lips. "There will never be a day that I don't thank the universe and every higher power for bringing you into my life. I love you, Ava Marie Schmidt. There is not a place you could go in this world that I would not find you. You are wholly and completely mine, and I am so excited to spend the rest of my life worshiping you, body and soul."

Epilogue

Vi

After years of preparation, I was finally about to attend my first practice at the New York ballet company, and my stomach was full of knots. Ava wanted to celebrate by going out for coffee before work, and where Ava was, Art was never far behind.

As usual, Art had invited Finn along, which was how I ended up sitting in a booth with Ava at our local coffee shop waiting for the boys to arrive.

"I am so incredibly proud of you, and I feel like I could explode with excitement at the thought of seeing you on that stage! My best friend, a professional ballet dancer, I absolutely knew this day would come."

I'd never been good at taking compliments, and today was no different. Instead, I deflected, "You better not let Art hear you say that or he'll get all moody."

She waved her hand dismissively. "He knows his place."

It had been a month since Ava's abduction, and she'd taken the job Kim offered and moved to the city with me. We'd found a three bedroom house to rent in that time, and I could count on one hand how many times Ava and Art had slept in

242

separate beds since. I was happy for them, I really was, but I also felt a pang of something when I looked at the way they were so utterly in love with each other.

"Speaking of knowing their place, where's Phil?"

I braced myself for a conversation I knew I was not going to enjoy. "He's busy today, he couldn't make it."

"Why am I not surprised."

"Ava—"

"How many times does he have to refuse to show up before you understand that he doesn't care, Vi?"

"Not everyone can have an ooey gooey love like you and Art."

"That's not what I'm saying. You don't have to have a love like me. But you should have any sort of love in your relationship. Not whatever he brings."

"He's not so bad."

"Yeah, which is exactly why he never comes to hang out with us or support you in any way."

"He's just busy. We have our own lives."

"Vi, I'm promising you there's someone out there who will love you like you deserve. Unlike Phil."

I was saved from answering when the boys arrived, and I inwardly let out a sigh of relief. There weren't many things Ava and I didn't agree on, but Phil was definitely one of them.

Per usual, the minute they were in the same room Art attached himself to Ava like Velcro. It would be sickening if they weren't so goddamn cute together. Finn dropped into the open chair next to me.

"Congrats on the big day!"

"Thank you," my smile was full of excitement. "And thank you so much for coming."

"Of course, I wouldn't miss it."

I glanced back to the lovebirds, who scooted out of the

booth. "We're gonna go grab a coffee, do you want anything, Finn?"

"I'll take a Carmel latte please," he turned to me, "do you want a sandwich or anything to go with your coffee?"

I swirled my straw as I shook my head. "I'm too nervous to eat anything right now, I'll stick with my drink, but thank you."

Art and Ava headed for the counter, and I went back to my drink, looking up at Finn as he cleared his throat nervously.

"I know it might not be great timing, but I've been thinking about it for a while, and I was wondering if you wanted to go out with me sometime?"

My heart twisted at the look of hope on his face. "Finn…" I started.

"I know it might be weird since our best friends are all in love and everything, but I promise I won't be weird if—"

I cut him off before he could finish his thought. "Finn, no, it's not that, I have a boyfriend."

"Oh." His face pinked as he glanced down at the table before looking up again with a grimace. "Sorry, I didn't know. Ava's never said anything about him."

"Yeah, him and Ava don't get along."

I could see questions linger in his gaze, but he gave me a lopsided grin. "Oh. Sorry, I didn't mean to overstep or anything."

I shrugged and gave him a smile, "You didn't know."

Ava and Art returned with the rest of the beverages, but my thoughts remained on my previous conversations. I'd been stuck in the same pattern, always waiting to take hold of what I wanted but never actually getting it. I had pushed Ava to be brave and open herself up to new opportunities, and maybe it was time for me to do the same.

Stay tuned for Vi and Finn's story coming soon.

Acknowledgments

To Jasmine and Anandi, who took a chance on my book when it was still in the very rough stages, I appreciate you and your faith in me more than you know. To Lesly and Tammy for being excited for me every time I updated you on my progress. To everyone who's ever encouraged me to keep pursuing my dreams of seeing my book on a shelf, I did it! And to Greg for being the greatest partner and always willing to support me whether that be listening to me brainstorm or scribbling down a random scene for me in the car. I don't know how I got so lucky to find you, but I thank Jesus every day that you're mine.